The LEGEND of FROG

WITHDRAWN FROM ESSEX LIBRARIES

D0414054

To Ruth

Guy Bass

To the Princes and Princesses in my life,
and my own personal Rarewolf, for putting up
with me and keeping me drawing

Oda

STRIPES PUBLISHING
An imprint of Little Tiger Press
1 The Coda Centre, 189 Munster Road,
London SW6 6AW

A paperback original
First published in Great Britain in 2014

Text copyright © Guy Bass, 2014
Illustrations copyright © Dynamo, 2014
Cover illustration copyright © Jonny Duddle, 2014

ISBN: 978-1-84715-388-3

The right of Guy Bass and Dynamo to be identified as the author
and illustrator of this work respectively has been asserted by them
in accordance with the Copyright, Designs and Patents Act, 1988.

All rights reserved.

This book is sold subject to the condition that it shall not,
by way of trade or otherwise, be lent, resold, hired out,
or otherwise circulated without the publisher's prior consent in
any form of binding or cover other than that in which it is
published and without a similar condition, including this
condition, being imposed upon the subsequent purchaser.

A CIP catalogue record for this book is
available from the British Library.

Printed and bound in the UK.

2 4 6 8 10 9 7 5 3 1

The LEGEND of FROG

Guy Bass

Stripes

Once Upon
the End of the World...

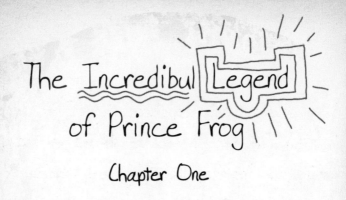

The Incredibul Legend of Prince Frog

Chapter One

One upon a tyme there was the KING AND QUEEN OF EVERYTHING. They rooled over all of Kingdomland and lived in a palase and had thrones and crowns and all the polished sandwitches they could eat.

Their palase looked really speshul and was chock-filled with loyal subjects. Their favourit loyal subject was called Buttercup who was good and clever and wize.

But the King and Queen of Everything were sad. They longed for a chilled child more than anything in the wurld. Then one day a golden egg appeered out of the lake in their garden. It was all shined-up and speshul looking and the King and Queen of Everything said great! A goldun egg! Soon it will hatch and owt will come a prince because that is where princes come from.

Then the wurld ended.

Buttercup said HEY LOOK EVRYONE THE WURLD IS ENDING LET'S GET OUT OF HERE AND LEAVE! But no one would lissen, not eaven the King and Queen. So Buttercup took the speshul goldun egg and she ran to the island at the edge of the end of the wurld to get away.

me

After the End of the Wurld happuned, Buttercup was all on her own and sad for ages. But then her goldun egg hatched and owt came a royal green prince.

Buttercup raized the prince like he was her own son. The prince was the <u>best and mightiest</u> prince. He grew up in no time flat. In one yeer he was strong and fast and he could jump highly on his mighty legs and had the cleverrest brain by a milliun and could make himself ~~camoflarged cammoflarjed~~ invisible like a magic ninja.

Except there was no Kingdomland or palase or servants bringing him crowns and polished sandwitches because the wurld was ended. The prince spent his hole life on a farty little island on the Edge of the End of the Wurld. His howse was not even a bit like a palase. It was small and had no thrones and all the prince had to eat was vegetabuls that tasted of burp. And he didn't get to see anything for real, only in the stories Buttercup toled him.

Then the prince thort what is the End of the Wurld like? So then he said to Buttercup please can I go and see what the End of the Wurld is like but Buttercup said NO! DON'T EVER EVER go to the End of the Wurld! It is all SCORTCHED EARTH and BLACKUNED SKYS and CATASTROFEE! She said it in that voice she only uses when she talks about the End of the Wurld. So the prince couldn't go and see what the End of the Wurld was like.

Which means he definitly can't tell Buttercup when he does.

I don't know what happens next. But I'll tell you when I get there.

The Island on the Edge of the End of the World

Frog replaced his quill pen in the inkpot. "Now for Chapter Two."

"What are you writing, Frog?"

Frog slammed his book shut. He turned to see Buttercup's head poking round the door. She looked nothing like Frog. She did not share his bright, mottled green skin or his bulbous yellow eyes. She had ears and a nose – which Frog lacked – and long, brown hair, while Frog had not a single hair on his head. In fact, Buttercup looked decidedly human – there wasn't a hint of anything amphibian about her. But then Buttercup had not hatched from a golden egg.

"I'm – uh – I'm just writing down our

story," replied Frog. "About the golden egg and the mighty prince."

"It's most royal of you to practise your quill-craft," she said, "but it's past both our bedtimes and we have a big day tomorrow: the flower needs watering, the potato needs picking, the clouds need counting…"

"We did all that yesterday – and the day before," huffed Frog.

"We could always practise your camouflage," Buttercup suggested.

"What do I have to hide from? There's no one here but us," said Frog, unleashing a loud and deliberate sigh. He hopped down from his chair and into bed.

"So, what story would you like?" said Buttercup, as she tucked him in. "I could tell you about the time I rode the Queen's newnicorns? Or the time the King out-farted the imp-O-lights? Or when the sunbirds gave the Queen a ray of light for her birthday?" She glanced at Frog's story. "Or about the golden egg that hatched a mighty prince…"

"You could tell me about the End of the World," Frog said.

"Again? There's nothing more to tell," Buttercup sighed, rubbing her eyes. "Scorched earth … blackened skies … catastrophe."

"Catastrophe," repeated Frog, in a reverie. "Does anyone live there?"

"Of course not," sighed Buttercup. "How could anyone live at the End of the World?"

"I don't know, it's just – I'm a prince," said Frog. "Do I really have to stay on this island forever? It feels like I'm meant for something more … princely."

Buttercup stiffened. She took a deep

breath and looked at her feet. By the time she looked up she had put on a smile. "What did you dream last night? Do you remember?" she asked.

Frog remembered his not uncommon dream immediately. "I was in the sky, higher than everything, higher than the stars, looking down on the world," he replied.

"Did it feel real?" she asked. Frog nodded. "So, can you fly higher than the stars?"

"No, but—"

"No. Just because you feel something doesn't make it real," said Buttercup quickly. "You were destined to be a great ruler, Frog – I'm sure you would have been. But that world is gone. The World has Ended. We and this island are all that is left. I brought you here and built you a home and kept you safe. It's just you and me, forever and ever."

"I know, but ... forever is ages," huffed Frog.

Buttercup let out a chuckle. "You're a good boy, Frog," she said, kissing him on the head.

Frog knew what she would say as she put out the lamp — she had said the same thing every night since he'd hatched from his golden egg.

"Sleep well, Royal Majesty, Lord of all Kingdoms, Rightful Ruler of the World ... Prince Frog."

The Storm

Two hours passed before Frog was sure Buttercup was asleep.

"Stay here forever? Pfff – not this prince," he whispered. He reached under his bed and pulled out a wooden box. From it he took all he would need on his journey to the End of the World: one pair of catastrophe pants.

Catastrophe Pants

Made of the most excellent best matereals EVER, CATASTROPHE PANTS combine princely fashun with apocalips-busting usability. With a pair of CATASTROPHE PANTS you get to say "no" to no-frills – you'll look stylish and sofisticated even when you're up to your nees in the End of the Wurld. CATASTROPHE PANTS...

For the prince on the move!

Following a moment's proud inspection, Frog put them on. They were an odd patchwork of mismatched, sewn-together materials. Not for the first time, Frog admired his reflection in the mirror.

"Looking good, Your Majesty," he said, puffing out his chest. Despite being little over a year old, Frog looked more like a boy of ten – though definitely a lot greener. His huge, yellow eyes blinked back at him and his broad smile spread across his entire face.

Time to address my loyal subjects, he thought. He turned to his table, upon which sat a crudely stitched teddy bear, a stuffed sock-snake with buttons for eyes and a rock with a face drawn on it. Frog cleared his throat and placed his hand on his heart.

"Goodly loyal citizens, the time has come for your prince to answer the call of destiny," began Frog. "The day is upon us – the day that I embark upon my royal adventure. I must brave the scorched earth and the blackened skies and the catastrophe … and see what the End of the World is like. But fear not, I shall return! And I'll bring you back something nice."

He waited a moment, imagining rapturous applause (since his "loyal subjects" remained unmoved). Then he returned to his bed and drew a short, gnarled stick from under his pillow.

"Basil Rathbone," he said. "No adventure to the End of the World would be complete without a mighty sword – and you are my most first-rate and unbreakable of top weapons. You will never leave my side …not even when I need a wee."

Frog slipped the stick into his belt and crept out of his room. On the way out of the house he put his head round the door to Buttercup's bedroom. She slept as soundly as ever – snoring like a drain. Frog tiptoed to the back door and opened it. The moon was a curved notch of light, whittled out of the black sky. He opened the back door. The Inbetween shimmered silver in the moonlight. This great expanse of water was all that lay between him and the End of the World.

Frog had only just stepped out of the door when he felt a familiar tingle in his long, webbed toes. He looked down and wiggled them. It could mean only one thing.

Frog glanced up at the sky. "Not now," he groaned. "The toes knows..."

kA-BOOOOOM!

Thunder clapped in the sky so loudly that he felt his teeth shake. The next moment, it was as if an ocean tumbled from the sky — rain fell in a great, heavy torrent and lightning struck the ground only a few paces from the house.

Frog looked back to check that the noise had not woken Buttercup ... but it seemed she really could sleep through anything. "*The storm is the End of the World trying to reach us,*"

Buttercup would tell him. But this was no time for Frog to shy away from his destiny – the rightful ruler of the world wasn't about to spend his whole life on a farty little island.

Frog took a deep breath and stepped out into the storm. He was immediately drenched from head to toe. He hurried round the back of the house, dodging the lightning bolts that forked down from the sky and battered the ground. He raced across the burp-smelling vegetable patch and down to the end of the garden. From under the largest and bushiest bush in the garden, he retrieved his Raft of Ideas. The raft was no more than five crudely bound logs with a makeshift sail, but Frog had spent weeks building it in secret and couldn't have been happier with the result.

"Yoiks!" Frog cried as a bolt of lightning lit up the ground only paces away. "Time to go!"

He dragged the raft to the edge of the Inbetween. The dark waters crashed against the shore as if trying to turn him back. Undeterred, Frog pulled the raft on to the water with an almighty heave and clambered on.

The raft was quickly buffeted across the water. After a few moments Frog looked back at the shrinking island, lightning striking its only tree.

"Just you and me now, Basil Rathbone," he said, holding his stick aloft. "Onward, to the End of the World! The adventure begins!"

The Inbetween

"The … adventure … is so … boooring!"

The raft had been floating serenely across the Inbetween for hours. The storm had long since passed and taken the night with it – the light of dawn illuminated the silvery stillness, stretching in all directions.

"Stupid Inbetween goes on forever!" continued Frog with a shrug. "We must be getting close to the End of the World by now; I thought at least things might be getting a bit choppy or bumpy or EXPLOOM! KA-FLAME! Where's the scorched earth? The blackened skies? Catastrophe?"

A breeze tugged lazily at the raft's sail and a whistle fish bobbed to the surface. It whistled a gleeful "wheet!" and then bobbed back under the water.

Frog called after it. "Hey! Which way to the End of the... Wuh?"

Something on the horizon caught his eye. A wave had began to swell as it moved slowly towards the raft...

"This is it! An apocalyptic tidal wave, the likes of which no one has ever seen!" he cried. "The first sure sign of the End of the World! Brace for impact!"

But the wave remained decidedly un-tidal and the raft bobbed gently as it passed harmlessly beneath them.

"What the ... what? What does a prince have to do to get a little End of the World around here?" growled Frog. "I might as well have stayed on the island if all I was going to see was— Wait ... what's that?"

Frog got to his feet as he looked out over

the Inbetween. A thick, grey wall swept across the water towards him. "OK, this time! The End of the World approaches! The Clouds of Catastrophe! Only the mightiest prince can possibly withstand its apocalyptic power!"

The wall of grey engulfed him — a damp cloud of harmless fog.

"Oh, come on! What's catastrophic about fog? I get fog at home!" Frog wailed as he sailed blindly through the gentle waves. "Did I not mention I'm the Prince of Everything? I want the End of the World and I want it right—"

The Raft of Ideas disappeared from under him. Frog screamed — but then he fell so far that he had to take a breath in the middle.

"NAAEEEEEEEEEEEEEEEEE - HUUUUR -AEEEEEEEEEEEEEEEEEEEEEEEEEEEEeeeeeeee

← Frog

The Waterfall in
the Sky

It took Frog a moment to remember how to breathe underwater. He was no longer in the calm waters of the Inbetween; a strong current was pulling him along and he could see banks of grass and hookweeds on either side of him – and below him a bed of sand. By the time he realized he must be in a river he was surrounded by whistle fish, darting around his head, gleefully *wheet!*-ing in the hope that he would play with them.

Frog let himself sink until he felt the ground beneath his feet. He pushed hard with his mighty legs and launched himself upwards, scattering the fish and darting back towards the surface. He burst out of the water and scrambled on to the bank, spitting out a mouthful of water and a whistle fish that he'd accidentally swallowed.

"What the … what?" Frog blurted. He rolled on to his back and peered upwards.

Water tumbled from a bright morning sky. It was a vast, roaring, vertical river, flowing in a torrent from nowhere – through the clouds and down for what looked like miles. Finally, it met with an unfeasibly high cliff and crashed into the base of a wide river. Frog was sitting on the river's bank, wet through.

"I must have fallen *forever*," he whispered, sitting up. A few logs bobbed past him in the river and he spotted his sail, tangled round a rock – all that remained of his Raft of Ideas.

Frog leaped to his feet and counted his

fingers and toes (a princely four on each hand and foot). Then he made sure that his trusty stick was still in his belt and checked his catastrophe pants for signs of catastrophe.

"Not a scratch..." he noted. "Ha! Forever isn't so far to fall. Call yourself catastrophic? Call yourself the End ... of the... Wuh?"

Frog looked around. The sky was a rich blue, and a fine spray of water from the falls created a sparkling rainbow in the air. Ahead of him, the shallow river shimmered with light and life and shoals of whistle fish, larger and more colourful than he had ever seen in the Inbetween, dancing out of the water as they dodged the hookweeds' flailing tendrils. Behind him, Frog saw lush forest, as green as his own skin and aching with fresh, dewy life. And beyond that, soft, rolling hills, tall trees and vast, snow-capped mountains...

"Wait, *is* this the End of the World?" he said. "Where are the scorched earth and the blackened skies and such? Did I take a wrong turn? Where——"

"Baa."

Frog turned, slowly.

There was a grubby mess of wool and legs staring back at him.

"Baa."

The Sheep

Buttercup had told so many stories of Kingdomland – painted so many pictures in Frog's mind of the world that had existed before the End of the World – that the woolly white creature that stared up at him seemed almost familiar.

"You're a sheep," he said.

"Baa," replied the sheep.

"An *actual* sheep."

"Baa," replied the sheep.

"Except … you can't be," Frog added. "I know there are no sheep at the End of the World; I know there aren't any *anythings* at the End of the World. And a prince knows what a prince knows. It is the second rule of princeliness:

The Rules of Princeliness

1. The Prince is Mightier than the Sord.
   He is also mightier than everything else,
   including giants

2. A Prince Knows what a Prince Knows.
   None shall queschun the wisdum of a prince.
   (Except Buttercup. She can tell him to tidey his
   room or go to bed or do his chors or finish his
   vejetables and no I don't care that it tastes like
   burp just eat it it's good for you)

3. Princes are good because
   goodness is princely

4. Princes must allways make
   the rite choice

5. Princes are green

"So, if there are no anythings at the End of the World, then you must be a figment of my— Hey!"

Frog looked down. The sheep had started to chew the stick on his belt.

"Stop that!" exclaimed Frog. "You do *not* nibble on the mightiest, most first-rate unbreakable sword in the world!"

"Baa?"

"That's all right, you weren't to know — you've probably never seen a top royal sword before. You've probably never even seen a proper *prince* before," Frog mused. He tugged up his catastrophe pants and puffed out his chest. "Well, look upon my greenness and know that I am Your Royal Majesty, Lord of all Kingdoms, Rightful Ruler of the World … Prince Frog!"

The sheep stared at Frog through blank eyes.

"Behold my mighty jumping legs!" Frog cried, showing off a skinny thigh.

The sheep continued to stare.

"Observe my princely power!" Frog continued, triggering his camouflage. The next moment, he seemed to disappear in front of the sheep's eyes. (Except for his catastrophe pants, which remained unmistakably visible.)

The sheep watched a spiderfly buzz round its head.

"And feast your eyes on my most royal of complexions – I'm green!" insisted Frog, reappearing. "I'm glorious, green Prince Frog!"

The sheep began chewing on a tuft of grass. Frog peered at it – then he looked at the teeth marks on his stick. An idea – an unimaginably significant idea – dawned

upon him. He reached out a long, green finger and poked the sheep on the nose.

"You are here, aren't you? I mean, you're actually, really, fully here. And if you're here…" Frog wrinkled his brow. He looked about again – and his eyes grew wide. "No scorched earth … no blackened skies … no catastrophe! The world *hasn't* ended after all!"

"Baa," the sheep added.

The Not-So-Ended World

"This is *definitely* going in my diary," said Frog, shaking his fists with excitement. The sheep cocked its head to the side. "Don't you get it, sheep? The world hasn't ended! Imagine the looks on people's faces when they realize their mighty Prince is all alive and well and ready to claim his rightful throne! I've got to tell Buttercup — she thinks it's scorched earth and so on. How do I get back up the waterfall in the sky?"

The sheep looked away, searching for grass to graze upon.

"I probably just need a magic talisman or something to get me up there; Buttercup said the un-ended world was *bursting* with magic business — the King and Queen even had their own skilled-up wizard." Frog looked up at the waterfall. "Unless — wait ... unless I claim my throne *first* and then send my loyal subjects to go and get Buttercup... They could collect her in my most excellent royal raft. Then she'd arrive at the royal palace to see me on my throne all crowned up and princely looking!"

Frog turned back to the sheep, which chewed on a thick clump of grass.

"You know, sheep, I could do with a guide to show me. Giddy! Giddy!" repeated Frog, kicking the sheep again. And again.

"Giddygiddygiddygiddygiddygiddygid dygiddygiddygiddygiddygiddygiddy!"

There was a pause in the proceedings while Frog pushed out a grumbling sigh. "Why aren't you giddying?"

"Baa," said the sheep.

"Hmm … you're probably intimidated by how extra princely I am," he mused, hopping off the sheep. "Don't worry, I'll show you the ropes. You'll be proper skilled up and steed-looking by the time we get to the palace. This way!"

Frog raced down the riverbank like an excited toddler. The sheep swallowed the bit of grass it was chewing and trotted after him.

Frog and his trusty steed, *Sheriff Explosion* (Frog had named his sheep to make it sound more impressive), made their way assuredly towards the palace. After all, how could a prince *not* find his way to his own palace?

The Not-So-Ended World was an almost unimaginably vivid and sprawling landscape, and Frog found himself unprepared for its majesty. The world was drenched in colours, textures, sounds and smells — an irresistible feast for Frog's keen senses. One moment, he was clambering through a dew-dropped forest, thick with the scent of pine and flowers — the next he found himself wandering through an arid desert, watching vulture-crabs fight noisily over bones. In the morning he crossed a rickety bridge over a vast lake of belching, purplish ooze — but by the afternoon he was striding atop a great mountainous gorge, a warm, golden-hued breeze settling on his skin in an aura of light as he stared down at swooping sunbirds.

"It's amazing," Frog replied, his eyes glistening with tears. "It's *so* much better than the island. *Seven* times more … or maybe a million. And it's all mine."

The Rarewolf

Frog and Sheriff Explosion clambered across a sea of smooth, weather-hewn rocks, covered in a shifting kaleidoscope of brightly coloured moss. They had been walking all day – the sun was beginning to dip behind the horizon.

Frog suddenly stopped. He looked down at his itching toes and gave them a wiggle. It was the same feeling he always got moments before the storm hammered the island. He stared up into the cloudless sky.

"Here comes the storm, Sheriff Explosion," he exclaimed. "My toes knows!"

kA-BOOOOOM!

"Baa?" the sheep bleated.

An ocean of water immediately fell from the sky. Frog watched lightning strike the ground in front of them. The sheep panicked and ran for the cover of a nearby outcropping.

"Don't worry, Sheriff – turns out it's not the End of the World," said Frog, retrieving his trusty steed. "At least, I'm pretty sure it's not. Come on."

Frog dragged Sheriff Explosion through the storm, impatient to continue to the palace, wherever it may be. They made their way down a deep ravine overlooked by tree-sprouting crags on either side. Then, in the distance, Frog saw the shape of a huge, unmoving creature. As lightning struck the ground behind it, the beast was silhouetted against the dwindling light of dusk.

"What is *that*?"

The great, grey beast took a few steps forward. It was a wolf – or as close to a wolf as any description Buttercup had given. It had four legs, thick, grey fur and a long, stern face ... but this beast was *huge* – bigger than any animal he had ever imagined. Frog barely came up to its underbelly.

As he stepped closer, Frog realized that the giant wolf's fur was dry – the raindrops did not touch it as they fell.

"Hello!" Frog cried. "Look upon my greenness and know that I am Your Royal Majesty, Lord of all Kingdoms, Rightful Ruler of the World – Prince Frog!"

He strode towards the creature and did not stop until he could feel the giant wolf's hot breath on his face. Its piercing, plate-sized eyes examined him with knee-weakening intensity. An impressed grin spread across Frog's face.

"Buttercup said that the King and Queen of Everything ride newnicorns," continued Frog, wiping the rain from his eyes. "That's basically just a horse with a horn… Think how mighty and excellent I'd look turning up to the royal palace riding *you*."

The wolf grunted – a low, guttural growl – and then *spoke*.

"I have been waiting for you," it said, its rumbling voice echoing down the ravine.

"You can talk! Great!" cried Frog. "Buttercup says that means you're either a person or a gobbin or an unfairy … or maybe the Lord of All Newnicorns."

The creature growled so loudly that Frog was blown back a step.

"I am a *rarewolf*," it said. "I am the *last* of the rarewolves."

"A one-off, eh? That makes you an even

better royal steed," Frog replied.

The rarewolf growled again, baring a set of intimidatingly sharp teeth. "Did you really imagine you could leave the island without me noticing?" it said. "I know all the secrets of this—"

"Except … I already *have* a royal steed," Frog interrupted. He pointed to his sheep, which shivered in the driving rain. "I know he's not much to look at – and he's not really got the hang of royal steeding yet – but it would be un-princely to go back on my word. I know you must be disappointed…"

"Turn back," the rarewolf snarled. "Return to the island – or suffer the consequences."

"Go back to the island? Not a pant's chance! I *just* got here," replied Frog. "Anyway, there's a shined-up throne and a bunch of loyal subjects waiting for me. D'you know the way to the royal palace?"

"Do not defy me!" The rarewolf lunged forward, teeth bared, mouth open. "I am a rarewolf! Guardian of the land! Lord of the storm!"

With that, thunder clapped in the sky and a lightning bolt struck the ground a few paces from where Frog was standing.

"Wait, are you *doing* this weather? That's pretty skilled-up magic," said an impressed Frog. "Hey, do you make *all* the storms? Did you make the ones on the island? Could you work some of that for when I arrive at the castle? For a proper dramatic entrance, I mean – KA-FLASH! FWA-THUNDER! Here comes Prince Frog!"

"I could just eat you," the rarewolf said. "Swallow you whole and be done with it."

"Pfff — eat a mighty prince? Good luck with that," scoffed Frog, taking his stick from his belt and waving it around. "I'd hand you your tail in three seconds flat. I'd bring so much defeat to your door that you'd have to move house!"

"You…" began the rarewolf, its teeth bared. After a moment it snorted loudly and turned away. "You cannot imagine the trouble you have caused."

"Trouble? You must have me confused with someone else — I've been stuck on a farty little island my whole life — it's hard to get into trouble when all you can do is count clouds," said Frog. "Well, not any more — it's all big, wide world from now on. I'm destined for greatness!"

"*Destined…*" repeated the rarewolf. It sighed and stared upwards. Within seconds the rain had stopped and the clouds began to part. "My brothers and sisters were right – no matter what I do, the prophecy unfolds."

"What prophecy?" asked Frog.

The rarewolf stared at him. "Sit down, child," he said, gesturing to a large rock next to him.

Frog rubbed his chin. "OK, but no funny business – I don't want to use up any of my mightiness before I get to the palace," he said, taking a seat. He slapped his hands on his knees. "So, are you going to tell me a story?"

"In a manner of speaking," the rarewolf replied. "It is the story of the End of the World."

The Prophecy

"The End of the World?" repeated Frog. "I already know this one! You don't need to worry – the world's not even ended. You know how I know? 'Cause there's stuff and things everywhere – look!"

The rarewolf sat slowly back on its haunches and looked up into the darkening sky. "Do you know, I have been waiting for this moment – waiting for *you* – for a thousand years."

"A thousand?" repeated Frog with a grin. "I must be the most important prince *ever*."

The rarewolf managed an amused snort. "We rarewolves were the first creatures, born in the first moments of the world," the rarewolf continued. "We were the guardians of the land and, in return, the land gave up its secrets to us – secrets of the past and the future. At first we thought it was a gift, but believe me, it is a great burden to know what is coming."

"Pfff – if I'd known the world was still here I'd have left that island a *yonk* ago," replied Frog. "I'd have been doing royal business left, right and centre. Just you wait till I get to the——"

"*Then* the day came when we foresaw the End of the World," added the rarewolf insistently. "A prophecy of doom. Scorched earth ... blackened skies——"

"Catastrophe!" interrupted Frog. "That's just what Buttercup said – she must have heard the same thing. She's going to feel like a burpy turnip when she finds out it's all still here." Frog looked back to Sheriff Explosion, waiting nervously behind a shrub. He gave the sheep a wink, drummed his fingers on his knees and went to get up. "Speaking of which, I have a throne to sit on, so…"

"The other rarewolves begged me not to interfere – they said that it would only lead to more destruction – but I had to do something," the rarewolf continued. "I went against their wishes and in doing so … I doomed them all."

"What did you do?" asked Frog, his interest suddenly piqued by talk of destruction and doom.

"I tried to save us! Am I not a guardian? What else could I do? It is not easy to leave the fate of the world to someone else," replied the rarewolf. It stared out across the ravine and watched the sun dip behind the horizon. "Others will try and decide *your* fate, Frog. But you must choose for yourself ... you must choose your own destiny."

"Wait, is that what this is about?" tutted Frog. "I *know* what my destiny holds. I'm going to find the royal palace and then it's all crowns and loyal subjects and polished sandwiches forever! Now are you going to point me to the royal palace or not?"

"Destiny, Frog ... the fate of the world," the rarewolf repeated, slowly and firmly. "It is in your hands."

"Which is *why* I'm trying to get to the palace," sighed an impatient Frog. "Destiny fulfilling is top of my to-do list..."

The rarewolf let out a long, resigned grumble. It pointed its great head to the sunset.

"A day's walk in that direction."

"Really? Great! Ho, Sheriff Explosion!"

said Frog. He barged past the rarewolf and his sheep hurried nervously after him.

"Listen for the thunder... Look for the lightning!" the rarewolf called after them. "I will help you, if I can ... but first you must choose."

"Thunder, lightning – got it!" called Frog, but in truth he was barely listening. He was one day away from the palace... One day away from his destiny.

The Palace

"Yesly, Yer Majesty...! What's biddings, Majesty...? Sandwiches, Majest—uh?"

Frog sat up with a start, princely dreams bouncing round in his brain. For a moment he thought he was back in his bedroom on the island. He could hear Buttercup singing in the garden and smell the burp of the vegetable patch wafting through his window. Then the loud buzz of a passing bumbleflea shook him back to reality. He rubbed his eyes.

The cave in which he and his sheep had slept overnight was warm and clammy. The walls were coated in a gooey film of luminous nectar that bathed the cave in a soft, blue light. Excitement fluttered in Frog's belly. He wondered what Buttercup would think if she

56

could see him now – here, in the Not-So-Ended World – and how happy she would be when she finally saw him on his rightful throne.

"Sheriff Explosion?" Frog said, looking around. He got up and stepped out into the morning light. "Sheriff? Where are you?"

The sun was breaking through the clouds and shining down on to a wide, fertile valley. Above, a great mountain stretched up into the sky, obscured by clouds at the top. Frog squinted in the sunlight and spotted his trusty steed at the foot of the mountain.

"Sheriff! Come back!" he cried. He raced after the sheep, crossing the valley in a few mighty leaps. Sheriff Explosion was gazing upwards as it chewed lazily on a mouthful of apple-green grass.

"You can't just run off like that, Sheriff

— a prince and his trusty steed have to stick together, no matter what," said Frog. "What if that stupid rarewolf started thundering and lightning-ing all over the place? You could be— What are you staring at?"

Frog looked up and his wide eyes grew even wider. "The palace... My palace!"

The clouds parted as if by royal command and bright sunshine streamed down upon the palace. It was magnificent. The imperial citadel stood proudly, as if it had sprouted from the top of the mountain like a majestic tree. Its walls were of a gleaming, pearl-white stone and a dozen lofty towers jutted into the sky, shimmering brightly.

"It's even *better* than Buttercup described," Frog whispered, a smile spreading across his green face. "It's incredible ... it's magical ... it's good to be *home*."

"Baa," said Sheriff Explosion.

"You said it. Let's go, mighty royal steed! Make with the giddying!" Frog cried, leaping on to the sheep.

Sheriff Explosion did not move.

"Fine," sighed Frog, hopping off, "but I'm giving you some proper royal steeding lessons once we get to the palace."

The climb to the palace was long and gruelling – and eventually Frog grew tired of coaxing or dragging Sheriff Explosion up the mountain. He hauled the sheep on to his back and began leaping up the mountain in great, long hops.

As soon as he reached the top, Frog spotted the majestically tall palace gates and sped towards them. He crossed a wide bridge, stretching out across a huge, dark chasm so deep that Frog could not see the bottom.

By the time he reached the gates, Frog was breathless. He put Sheriff Explosion down, panting heavily, as two sentries in impractically cumbersome armour clunked and clanked in front of his path, crossing their spears.

"Halt!" cried one of the sentries. "Oh, you have."

"The wait ... is over!" gasped Frog. "I am he ... His Royal Majesty, Lord of all Kingdoms, Rightful Ruler ... of the World ... Prince Frog!"

The sentries turned to each other.

"What is it – some sort of moss-gobbin?" asked one.

"Could be a bog urchin," said the other.

"Would you just let me in?" continued Frog. "Don't you know a prince when you see one?"

"None may enter the palace of Kingdomland!" roared the sentries. One added, "Except by royal invitation of His Kingliness the King and Her Queenliness the Queen! Or unless they've brought another newnicorn for the princess."

"What are you on about? I just said—" began Frog. "Wait, did you say *princess*?"

"That's Her Most Tremendously Royal Princess Rainbow to you, gobbin," noted the other sentry.

"What are you—? There is no princess! There is only me! Prince me! I mean, Prince Frog!" snapped a flustered Frog, striding towards them. "Who is this pretend princess? Let me in! I demand to see her!"

The sentries clacked their spears together in defiance.

"None shall pass!" they cried.

"Pfff — don't say I didn't warn you," said Frog smugly. He drew his stick from his belt. "Prepare to face Basil Rathbone!"

Basil Rathbone

Having a mighty sord is super importunt if yor a Prince. Even though Princes are mighty enuff to beat everyone in the wurld with their bear hands it might take a million years. A mighty sord makes beating everyone ten times easier. Basil Rathbone was forged by the most skilled-up sword maker ever and is so first-rate and magically unbreakable it can chop through anything. Only to be wielded by the most excellent top skilled-up prince in the wurld.

"You're about to get a bath full of hot defeat tipped on your heads," replied Frog, brandishing the stick in front of their faces. "And I'm running the bath!"

The guards began to chuckle. Then laugh. Then guffaw, falling about with unconcealed merriment. But at the precise moment that the guffawing was at its most unbridled – it suddenly stopped. In an instant, the guards' expressions turned to icy terror.

"Oh, no … no, no, no!" shrieked one guard. "R-r-rare—"

"R-run!" squealed the other.

The guards threw their spears to the ground and frantically opened the palace gates. They sped through as fast as their clanking armour could carry them, shouting, "It's happening again! Sound the alarm!

The alarm! Sound it!"

"Yep, you'd better run!" he said. "Come on, Sheriff Explosion!"

Frog strode inside. His sheep turned slowly back and peered down the bridge. At the other end, silhouetted against the bright morning light, was the rarewolf. It nodded to Sheriff Explosion, who let out a nervous bleat and followed Frog inside.

"Don't let me down, prince," said the rarewolf — then it turned to leave. "Prophecies ... nothing but trouble."

The Throne

"Pfff – 'princess' indeed!" Frog huffed, as he strode down the grand marble corridors of the palace, Sheriff Explosion trotting nervously behind. "How long has this *imposter* been playing with my rightful stuff and messing up my royal things? She'd better not be sitting on my throne…"

Frog barely noticed the breathtaking majesty of the palace's interior as he searched for the throne room. He ignored the golden statues, the polished marble pillars, the grand, intricate tapestries … the room that had nothing but a big slide in it. Frog pressed on, barging past servants and handmaidens, officials and dignitaries, guards and watchmen, all of whom muttered in confusion at the appearance of this disturbingly green visitor.

"Where is it?" cried Frog, finding himself in a vast, open courtyard lined with perfectly spherical trees in every imaginable colour. "Where's the throne room?"

He raced down another corridor into a hall that seemed to be made entirely of gold. At the end of the hall was a door, as high as Frog's house. Frog ran towards it and pushed it with all his might.

The door swung open.

"Sheriff Explosion, we've found it!"

The royal throne room was long and grand – and empty but for a wide gilded staircase leading up and up. There, at its summit, framed with cascading crimson velvet and polished to a glorious sheen, were three thrones. "Baa," said an impressed Sheriff Explosion.

Frog walked slowly towards the foot of the steps. He took a deep, long breath and climbed the stairs. He reached the top and examined each throne in turn.

"Too big … too big… Bingo."

My Throne
A Poem by Prince Frog

My throne is best of all the chairs
There's nothing speshul that compares.
I bet it will be regal green
And princely royal polished cleen.
I bet it fits my bottom rite
Not too loose, but not too tite.
All my subjects will neel down
And one will fetch my royal crown.
They'll put it on my hed and say
Hail Prince Frog! Hips hips hooray!

"My throne…" Frog whispered, staring at the smallest but finest golden seat.

It was a moment he thought would never — *could* never — come. His skin tingled with excitement and the rest of the world seemed to disappear. This was his birthright. His knobbly green knees trembled as he bent to sit…

"Intruders!" came a cry, as a dozen guards charged into the room, spears in hand.

"Baa!" cried Sheriff Explosion, as the guards surrounded him.

"Shut up, you! No bleating unless you're bleated to!" cried the captain.

A moment later an old man with a ridiculously long moustache and unfeasibly tall hat swept into the room.

"Gah!" cried the old man, gathering his robe in horror, as he fixed his stare upon the sheep. "Who let *that* in here? It'll mucky up the whole throne room!"

"We're not sure what's afoot, Lord Oldasdust – the palace is in uproar," replied the captain. "The sentries made claim of a rarewolf at the palace gates – as if such a thing is possible! Now folks are sayin' they've seen a *gobbin* wandering round the palace…"

"Gobbins? *Rarewolves?* My *omen hat* is getting tighter by the minute," wheezed Lord Oldasdust. "But where—"

"Loyal subjects! The wait is over!" came a cry.

Oldasdust and the guards peered up at the throne – and a uniform look of horror spread across their faces.

"What…"

"Is…"

"*That?*"

"That's right, it's me," nodded Frog, his hands on his hips. "Look upon my greenness and know that I am Your Royal Majesty, Lord of all Kingdoms, Rightful Ruler of—"

"Gah!" cried Oldasdust. "Get that ... *thing* away from that throne! Don't let its foul buttocks touch the royal seat!"

"Foul — what? Is everyone in Kingdomland colourblind? I'm green!" said Frog, pointing to his face. But before he could say another word, the guards had flung their spears at him.

"Yoiks!" cried Frog. He pushed off his mighty legs and sprang upwards. He landed halfway down the golden steps and hopped again, taking his stick out of his pocket as he spiralled in the air. He landed a single step in front of Oldasdust and their eyes met.

"What's wrong with you?" said Frog,

shoving his stick up Oldasdust's right nostril. "Don't you know a prince when you see one?"

"Gah!" cried Oldasdust, stumbling backwards. He reached into a pocket of his robes and took out a small piece of carved stone. "Foul gobbin! None may intimidate the royal wizard!"

With that, he cast the stone talisman to the ground. It exploded like a firework, creating a blinding shockwave that sent Frog stumbling backward into the guards. Before he knew what was happening, Frog felt himself being manhandled to the ground.

"What the ... what?" he muttered, his head spinning. He looked up to see the guards surround him, their swords inches from his slender, green neck. As he gripped his stick tightly, readying himself for battle, he heard the sharp *klik-klak* of tiny heels on the white marble floor.

"What's going on?" squeaked a mouse of a voice.

"Your Majesty, stay back!" Oldasdust cried. "There's badness afoot! The common herd has infiltrated the most royal of rooms!"

"I want to see! Let me see!" said the mouse voice again.

Lying on the ground with swords pressed to his neck, Frog could only see the bottom of the old wizard's robes. Then, with a *klik-klak*, something pushed past them and appeared before him.

"Hello. I'm five and three-quarters," it said.

It was her. It had to be. The pretend princess.

"Your breath smells like turnips," she said.

The Princess

"You are *not* a princess!" cried Frog, as he lay pressed against cold stone, half a dozen guards looming over him.

A gasp rang out across the throne room as he eyeballed the imposter.

The pretend princess didn't look anything like a *real* princess. She wasn't even green — but rather pink and as round as a pebble. Her face was plump and so rosy that it looked like she'd been standing in a gale. She wore a glittering, sugar-pink dress, sprinkled with diamonds. Her strawberry-blonde hair fell in ringlets and atop it sat a gleaming tiara.

"Your eyes are really big," she said with cheerful curiosity.

"Shall we lock the gobbin in the Tower of

Tallness, Your Majesty?" asked a guard.

"Or throw him in the Dungeon of Dread," suggested another. "The one that smells like old socks dipped in cheese on a hot day."

"Smells more like a cow eating rotting broccoli out of a sack full of old witch's farts," added another.

"*Or* we could just run him through," suggested the captain, his blade hovering over Frog's neck. "I just sharpened my stabby sword today…"

"Try it!" Frog replied. "I'll cook up an all-you-can-eat buffet of defeat and feed it to you!"

"Gah! Show some respect, gobbin!" shrieked Oldasdust. "You are in the presence of the Most Tremendously Royal Princess – Monarch of the Eastern Mountains and the Western Upside-downtains, Duchess of the

Dawn, Ruling Royal from the high, frozen plains of Refrigia to the undermost hillocks of the Eastern Hintercounties … the one and only Princess Rainbow!"

"I've got twenty dresses just like this one," said the princess, twirling round.

"Are you all blind? She is *not* a princess!" yelled Frog. "Now let me up this minute or I'll unleash my mightiness!"

Silence fell across the throne room.

"You're funny," said the princess and the smallest of titters fluttered out of her mouth. "I'm going to keep you as a pet. I'll call you Greeny, because you're green."

"Now, Princess, I *really* don't think—" began Oldasdust.

"A pet?" howled Frog. "I'm a prince!"

"Silly pet," the princess said. She turned to the wizard. "Oldasdust, get my champ'un to bring Greeny along – I want him to meet my other pets."

With that, the princess *klik-klak*-ed out of the throne room into the courtyard.

"But ... but ... *fine*," Oldasdust sighed. "Sentry! Blow the horn! Summon the Champion! Our greatest warrior, the royal protector, the heroic barbarian ... Man-Lor!"

The captain blew hard on his horn, filling the throne room with a resounding blare. Barely a moment later, from behind the throne, there emerged a figure of impractically huge dimensions. He was impossibly burly and muscular, and clad in little more than a furry loincloth and chainmail harness.

Man-Lor stepped forward, each of his well-oiled muscles straining like a balloon close to bursting.

"I ... am ... Man-Lor," he boomed, with such gravitas that the whole room seemed suddenly heavier.

"We know who you are, Man-Lor," sighed Oldasdust. "What were you doing hiding behind the throne?"

"...Toilet," admitted Man-Lor.

"Gah! This is the royal throne room!" snapped Oldasdust. With another sigh he added, "Just take this gobbin and go with the princess. I shall join you momentarily."

"I am Man-Lor," said Man-Lor. He reached behind him and drew a broadsword that was as big as Frog himself.

As the guards backed away, Frog got to his feet, straightened up and rolled his neck until it cracked. The bulging, brawny barbarian stood over him.

"Call that a sword, you great swollen lump of lumps?" Frog said with a wide grin. He held his stick aloft. "Now *this* is a sword. Prepare to eat defeat!"

The Hall of Kings

Frog awakened to find himself being carried, upside down, through the palace.

"What the— *Oww* ... what?" cried Frog, his head bumping along the ground. He looked up and saw Man-Lor's great hand wrapped round his left ankle. He checked his hand to find he was still clutching his mighty weapon. It had been snapped down the middle – one half clung loosely to the other.

"Basil Rathbone!" Frog cried. "You're meant to be unbreakable! *I'm* meant to be unbeatable! What happened to all my mightiness?"

Frog looked behind him (as best he could while upside down) to see if Sheriff Explosion was following ... but there was no sign of him.

"Sheriff Explosion!" he cried. "Stay alive, I will find you!"

Frog's strapping captor pushed open a large, heavy door and Frog found himself in a long, golden chamber, with impressively imposing portraits lining every wall. As he craned his neck to look, the chubby face of Princess Rainbow appeared in front of him.

"This is called the Hall of Kings, Greeny," said the princess, skipping down the long hall. "These are all the kings and queens and princes and princesses from ages and ages all the way until now."

"Princes? Let me see!" cried Frog.

"You're great – I've never had a pet that speaks," noted Princess Rainbow. She leaned into Frog until he could smell her floweriness. "But you can't ever speak when other people are around or they'll make

me get rid of you … and prob'ly cut your head off."

She skipped away to a portrait of an old man wearing ornate armour and an impressive crown. There was nothing even slightly green about him.

"Here's my daddy," she continued. "My daddy's the King of Everything! He's conq'ring the Land of Ice Gobbins right now.

It's hard when you're King of Everything because people keep saying, 'You're *not* the King of Everything!' so he has to bash them on the head until they say, 'OK, you *are* the King of Everything.'"

"How can that be the King of Everything? He's not even green!" shouted Frog, trying to get a look at the portraits as Man-Lor bumped him along the ground.

"And this is my mummy and she's the Queen of Everything," continued Princess Rainbow, pointing at a portrait of a woman with long, copper hair and a golden dress, holding the most impressive sword Frog had ever seen.

Princess Rainbow let out a sigh and added, "She likes going out conq'ring even more than Daddy, so I don't see her very much."

"Queen-shmeen! She isn't green either!" protested Frog. "You don't know the first thing about royalty, Princess *Brain-slow*!"

Princess Rainbow giggled at her new pet's silliness, stopping in front of the largest and grandest painting in the hall. "This is my favourite painting. It's Mummy and Daddy and me when I was four and three-quarters."

Something about the huge portrait immediately caught Frog's eye — apart from the fact that no one was even remotely green: Rainbow was cradling something in her arms.

"The golden egg…" said Frog, staring

wide-eyed at the painting. "That's my egg! What are you doing with my egg?"

"That's not an egg, silly," replied Princess Rainbow. "That's my golden ball. I saw it float up out of the lake in *my* back garden. Mummy and Daddy let me keep it. But then—"

"Ha! Shows what you know! That *is* an egg! I know it's an egg 'cause I hatched out of it, 'cause that's how royal folks get born. You don't know anything about royal *anything*. I bet you didn't even hatch out of an egg!"

"Silly Greeny — princes and princesses don't come out of eggs," replied the princess, wagging a stubby finger. "And they're not never, *ever* green — look."

The princess pointed to the numerous portraits in the Hall — kings, queens, princesses and princes. She was right.

None of them were green. Not one.

"Trees are green and grass is green and frogs are green," added Princess Rainbow. "And that's what you are. You're my pet frog."

The Curse of a Vivid Mind

The Chamber of Pets was a bright, grand room, with walls covered in gemstones and filled with ornate, decorated cages ... but it smelled worse than Frog's vegetable patch. It was teeming with an army of less-than-house-trained animals – crystal cats, diamond dogs, glamsters, even a tall, blue-feathered postrich...

...And one tiny green creature at which Frog could not help but stare.

"Ribbit."

"See? Mr Hoppy is a frog, just like you," said the princess, holding the frog in her hands. Man-Lor stood over them, staring into space.

"A frog? I've never seen— I've never even

heard of one of these … things before," Frog muttered. He never even knew "frog" was the name of an animal. He always thought it was just an excellent prince's name. But he did look a *lot* like this tiny creature. There was a ball of doubt in Frog's stomach – and it was growing heavier by the second.

"What's going on?" he muttered, as he peered at the frog. "Am I *Frog* … or *a frog?*"

"I like that you can talk," said the princess. She let out a small, sad sigh. "I wish my other pets could talk."

"Of course I can talk! I'm a whole year old," insisted Frog.

"That makes me four and three-quarter years older than you," said Princess Rainbow. "Maybe you're a *magic* frog. Did you really hatch out of the golden ball?"

Frog didn't answer – he was already

beginning to wonder why the idea of a prince hatching out of an egg seemed so ridiculous to her.

"Do you know Buttercup?" he asked the princess. "She was a loyal subject here until the End of the— Until a while ago."

Frog saw a flash of recognition in the eyes of the princess. She put her fingers to her lips.

"That's a bad name," she whispered. "You're not supposed to talk about Buttercup."

"What? Why not? What are you on about?" asked Frog.

"Promise to be my pet and my best friend and only to speak to me and not to anyone else," replied the princess conspiratorially, "and I'll tell you about Buttercup."

"What? I'm not promising you anything!

Just tell me!" Frog growled.

"Shhh!" whispered Princess Rainbow, putting her finger to her lips. "He's coming!"

"Your Majesty!" came a cry, as the door to the Chamber of Pets swung open. A breathless Oldasdust strode into the room, ducking as he entered to avoid knocking off his giant hat.

"Please pardon the intrusion," Oldasdust continued. He straightened his robes and adopted a stiff, ceremonial stance. "As you know, Your Majesty, the King and Queen have charged me – their most trusted royal wizard – with ensuring your safety while they are away on their conquests. Indeed, I have served the royal family for many a long, long year." He eyeballed Frog, as he stroked his long moustache. "Your parents were quite clear about the rules before they left – you

may not keep anything that *speaks*."

"But—" the princess began.

"The King and Queen don't want you filling your head with words – with *ideas* unbecoming of a princess," added the wizard.

"*But* Greeny doesn't speak. He's a frog," the princess insisted. She turned to Frog and gave him a wink. "He's a frog and frogs don't speak, so you must have imagined it."

"The curse of a vivid mind!" the wizard tutted. "I am quite certain I heard—"

"Well, you didn't. Did he, Greeny?" interrupted the princess.

Frog narrowed his eyes. "Of course I speak! This pretend princess is filled up with lies!" he cried defiantly.

"Gah!" cried Oldasdust. "You see, Princess? The gobbin speaks!"

"I teached him!" said the princess quickly. "He doesn't really speak — he just copies, like a chatterbird." She turned to Frog, a look of desperation flashing across her face. "Say something silly like I teached you, Greeny…"

"My name is *Frog*! Frooooooog!" he roared.

"See?" said Princess Rainbow.

"I'm sorry — I really am," admitted Oldasdust. "But this only *proves* why your parents do not allow you to have friends."

"Mummy and Daddy aren't here," said Princess Rainbow defiantly. "Only they can tell me what I can't have and if you cut Greeny's head off before they come back, I'll tell them that you let a *gobbin* into the palace."

"But, Princess—" began Oldasdust.

"Now I'm going to have a tea party with my pets," concluded the princess, "and *old* people aren't invited."

She nodded to Man-Lor, who obediently ushered Oldasdust out of the room. The wizard protested with a series of "but-but-but"s, but the door was quickly shut in his face.

"Bad Greeny!" snapped Princess Rainbow. "Now when Mummy and Daddy get back you're definitely going to get your head chopped off!" She took off her tiara with a sniff and threw it to the floor in front of Frog. "And I still won't have anyone — not anyone in the whole palace — who I can actually *talk* to."

"I am Man-Lor," said Man-Lor sadly.

"Oh, boo hoo! Poor, spoiled Princess Brain-slow has no friends!" scoffed Frog. "I … don't … *care*. Now tell me about Buttercup!"

The princess's round cheeks went even ruddier than usual. She blew air out of her nose, barely able to contain her rage.

"Fine," she grimaced. "Buttercup … was a *thief*. She stole my golden ball and I was sad. My mummy said if she ever saw Buttercup again, she'd cut her thieving head off with a big sword. Then Mummy said, 'Don't cry, things are just things, they're not important.' And then she got me another newnicorn."

"What are you talking about?" blurted Frog. "Buttercup didn't steal— The World … was … ending…" Frog trailed off, his mind befuddled with confusion and uncertainty.

Princess Rainbow eyed him thoughtfully. She considered leaving it there — but Frog had ruined her one chance to have a real, talking friend. She folded her arms and ground her teeth.

"If Buttercup told you that you're a prince, then she's a big, fat liar-head, because you're not. You're not *anything*. You're just a silly frog that came out of a ball, that came out of a lake. So there."

Frog felt the blood rush to his head. *Just a silly frog?* he thought. *Why would Buttercup tell me I was a prince? Why would she lie?*

The curse of a vivid mind. The wizard's words repeated in Frog's head. It suddenly felt as if he had imagined his entire life.

The Distracting Miracle of Death and Rebirth

Frog had spent three days in a cage as the princess's pet. She was so annoyed with him for speaking when he shouldn't that she locked him away in the Chamber of Pets and refused to visit. Twice a day, Man-Lor the barbarian arrived in the chamber and distributed notably unpolished sandwiches to the animals. Frog's loud protestations fell on deaf ears. "Let me out, Lumps!" he would cry. "I am Man-Lor," came the reply.

The first day was spent in a stupor of confusion and rage. Why would Buttercup lie to him about who he was? Even if she was no more than a thief — even if she had stolen the golden egg thinking it was treasure — why tell him he was a prince if he wasn't? Why let him spend all that time thinking he was important, when he was no better than the pets that now stared at him through vague, stupid eyes?

Frog wondered if that was why the rarewolf had told him to go back to the island – to spare him the humiliating truth. Because if he was not a prince, it might as well be the End of the World.

Frog spent the second day staring at his broken stick. Suddenly, he could see how plain and brown and gnarled and stick-like it looked. It was no more Basil Rathbone, his mighty sword, than he was a prince. How could he have been so childish?

Frog awoke on the third day with a single question gnawing at his brain – if he was not a prince, what was he? A frog, or something else? One thing was certain – the answer did not lie within his cage. For that, he would need to find the place of his "birth" – the lake.

It was then Frog had an idea.

"I am Man-Lor!"

It had been two hours since Frog's idea. Man-Lor strode into the Chamber of Pets carrying a plateful of sandwiches. He pushed the food through the diamond dogs' bars.

"Bark, doggies, bark," said Man-Lor.

"Tweet! Tweet!" yapped the bejewelled hounds in the opposite cage.

Man-Lor gurgled a laugh and turned to Frog's cage. "Bark, Greeny, bark," he said. But the still-locked cage was empty except for a pair of catastrophe pants. "Greeny?"

Man-Lor opened the cage and looked inside.

"Where are you, Greeny?" He lifted the open cage into the air and examined it from all angles. "Bad, bad, bad. Princess spank Man-Lor."

Stupid Lumps, I should have kicked him in the loincloth, thought a naked Frog as he raced through the palace. It had taken all his concentration to keep himself invisible inside the cage long enough to trick the barbarian into opening the door so that he could sneak out … but it was even harder to maintain his camouflage against the ever-changing background of the palace. Fortunately, he hardly saw anyone as he hurried through halls and corridors in search of escape — only a few servants milled around.

Before long, he had found his way outside into the magnificent, stately gardens at the rear of the palace. The gardens were bursting with life and colour and manicured with breathtaking artistry. Meticulous topiary and majestic sculptures punctuated bright, trimmed lawns and proud postriches strutted around the grounds, hissing and cawing like they owned the place.

Beyond the garden, Frog saw it: a large open lawn and a vast, silvery lake.

"The lake…" he whispered.

Frog crept down the garden, working hard to maintain his camouflage. After a moment he spotted a large crowd between him and the lake. They were staring at a herd of brightly coloured newnicorns. In the centre he saw the princess, sitting atop the shoulders of the old wizard.

"Behold the miracle of magic!" began Oldasdust, struggling to keep the princess on his head. "The newnicorns are dying to give birth!"

Buttercup had often spoken of the royal newnicorns. Each new moon morning the newnicorns died and gave birth to themselves. Frog was struck by how much more unpleasant the process was in real life than in Buttercup's stories. He felt rather queasy as the agonized cries of the dying newnicorns gave way to mewling wails of newborn foals.

Still, it was suitably distracting; Frog made his way invisibly through the transfixed crowd – ducking, weaving and crawling under legs until he was in the clear. He emerged to find himself no more than fifty paces from the lake.

"Greeny gone!" came a cry. "Don't spank Man-Lor!"

Frog spun round to see Man-Lor stamping down the garden towards the crowd.

Then: "AaaAAah! Naked gobbin!" cried a servant. Frog looked down. He had lost concentration – and his camouflage.

"That's my pet! Catch him, champ'un!" cried the princess from atop Oldasdust's hat.

"Yoiks…" Frog muttered. He turned on his heels and raced towards the lake. He ran so quickly that he occasionally sprang into the air, hopping across the gardens with ever-increasing speed and momentum. He startled a postrich, which snapped at him as he sped past. He had almost reached the shores of the lake when he suddenly panicked. What if he didn't like what he found? What if there was nothing princely about him at all? What if there was a family of lowly frog-gobbins down there, pining for their lost egg? Would he be happy being a frog-gobbin?

But Frog was already running too fast to stop – and he was not one to shy away from his destiny.

He leaped into the air... ("No, Greeny! Man-Lor no swim!") ... And dived headlong into the unknown.

The Secrets of the Lake

Frog took a few deep, long breaths of water and looked around. The lake was teeming with fish, the likes of which he had never seen. Spiked eels with unruly, flapping tails … fat, round gulpers with fins like whirring hummingbird wings … schools of whistle fish that had grown bigger, brighter and uglier than he thought possible … even the hookweeds that whipped out from the banks were larger and faster than he'd ever seen. Perhaps there *was* something magical about this lake.

Frog swam deeper, past the hordes of fish and foliage. Soon the waters of the lake grew dark and the fish disappeared but for a scant few glowing gulpers.

Before long the gulpers vanished too and the darkness became impenetrable. Frog continued to swim, down and down, feeling the pressure of the water grip him.

Turn back, he thought. But he kicked his legs as hard as he could, diving deeper into the inky depths.

Then he spotted it.

A green light, pulsing slowly in the distance. Then another, and another.

The deeper he swam, the more lights he saw. They were so bright that Frog could soon see quite clearly. He had at last reached the lake bed – it was dark and smooth, with lights covering it in every direction. Frog reached out to touch it. It was cold and metallic, like the bars of his cage. To his surprise, the lake bed shifted and opened at his touch, leaving a small, perfectly spherical hole in the ground.

Green light poured forth. It felt like an invitation.

Frog swam inside.

He found himself in a long, cylindrical corridor, illuminated green and made from the same dark, oily metal as the lake bed. The corridor soon gave way to a wide chamber, with what looked like mirrors on every wall. Frog swam through chamber after chamber, corridor after corridor. After a while he noticed something new — the faint glow of red light among the green. He followed the glow into a large, oval chamber and found the source — a bright orb of intense, red light, shining like a tiny star in the centre of the room.

Like a buttermoth to a flame Frog floated towards it, his hand outstretched — and brushed it with the tips of his fingers.

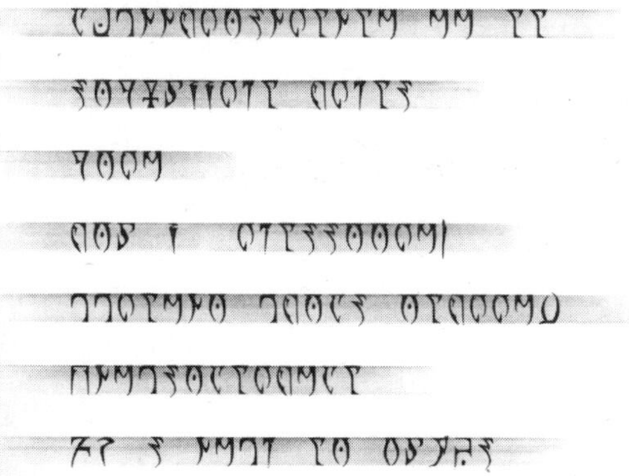

What the … what? thought Frog, pulling his hand away. The moment he touched the light it was as if a hundred bumblefleas started buzzing in his brain … as if his head wasn't big enough to contain them.

He went back for more – poking a finger into the light.

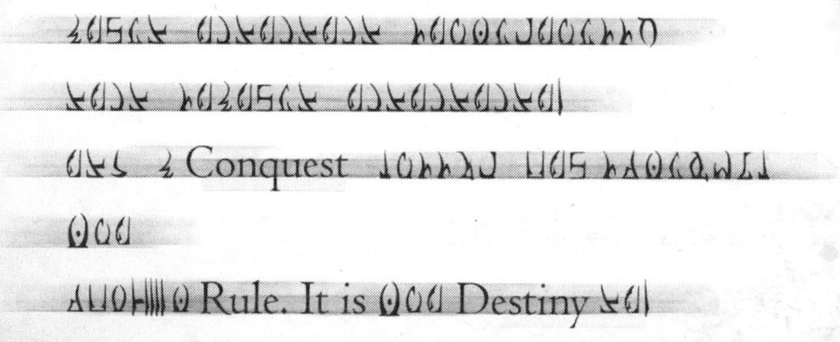
Conquest
Rule. It is
Destiny

He pulled away again. *What is... Did I understand that?*

This time Frog grabbed the ball of red light with both hands.

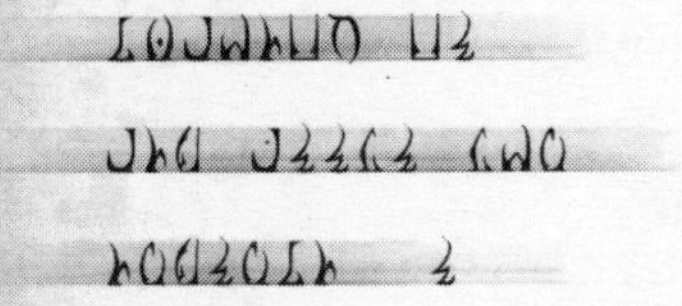

ᒪᘯᒍᘮᖹᕼᑌᘯ ᑌ�

ᒍᖹᘮ ᒍᕯᕯᕼᕯ ᕼᘯᘮ

ᖾᘮᘮᕯᘮᒪᖾ ᕯ

Contact

All at once, Frog felt as if a door in his brain was being prised open and a torrent of images rushed into his mind — a tidal wave, a great flood of blackness — as if the whole world had been poured into his head. He saw swirls of churning colour rush towards him ... and stars, hundreds of stars, bright and hot and close enough to touch. He closed his eyes to block it out, but there was no way of stopping it. He tried to picture the island ... Buttercup ... lying on his back on the shores of the Inbetween, counting clouds … but those memories had been pushed aside. All he could see in his mind's eye was a large, dark green orb, in the centre of pitch blackness. The orb turned slowly as it moved closer and closer. Soon, Frog could see it contained seas, islands, great masses of land and water… It was a whole *world*. He watched it slowly spinning in the starry sky.

Hail Kroak, said a voice in his head. Then…

Activating bipods.

The Army of a Thousand Sons awakens.

A second later, Frog heard a rumble as loud as thunder – and everything went from green to red.

The Bipods

Half the palace (and a herd of newnicorn foals) was gathered on the edge of the lake when Frog burst out of the water and crashed on to the grass. He lay there, panting, as Princess Rainbow stepped out of the crowd.

"Bad Greeny … now you'll prob'ly have your head cut off and *then* you'll be sorry." She crossed her arms with a disgruntled tut. "Did you bring me back any treasure?"

"Something … down there…" Frog gasped, "…coming … here!"

The princess eyed him suspiciously. "No treasure at all?" she huffed. "Not even one golden ball?"

Frog didn't answer. He stared at the lake as it suddenly glowed red and began to boil.

Within moments, a hundred helpless whistle fish rose to the surface of the lake, their dying *wheet*s filling the air.

"My fishies!" cried Princess Rainbow, her hands on her hips as she watched the lake bubble and churn. "What happened to my fishies?"

The answer came in a black shape emerging from the bubbling water. It was curved and smooth, like the clamshells on the shores of the island, but *vast* — as big as a house and made from the same oily, black metal that Frog had found at the bottom of the lake. With a grating whirr, the shape continued to rise until it was clear of the water, and Frog saw it was supported by two long, writhing metallic tendrils. It rose further, until it was taller than the tallest tree in the garden.

"Is that my treasure? It doesn't *look* like treasure," said Princess Rainbow.

Two more clamshell shapes rose slowly out of the lake behind the first, water, hookweeds and dead fish sloughing off them.

"I don't think it's treasure," murmured Frog. He stared up at the foremost clamshell and saw a red light flash across its surface. A moment later came the sound of hot steam escaping from a boiling pot … and it began to *open*.

"Is the treasure inside?" squeaked the princess excitedly.

"Would you shut up about treasure?" Frog snapped. He peered up as light and smoke poured out of the giant clamshell. Then a long, oily tongue snaked out from inside and curved towards the shore. As it finally touched the ground, Frog realized it was not a tongue, but a narrow flight of stairs.

"Gah! What dark sorcery is this?" hissed the wizard Oldasdust.

From the fog a giant figure emerged. It walked slowly down the steps, and Frog noticed how tall it was – even taller than the hulking Man-Lor. The giant was armoured from head to toe, but this wasn't some cumbersome combination of iron and chainmail – this armour comprised slick, interlocking plates, as smooth as polished stone. On its right leg was a holster with a large, red handle curving out and upon its head, a shiny black helmet covering its entire face.

"Yoiks…" Frog muttered, as the figure stopped directly in front of him. It reached a three-fingered hand to its face and prised the helmet from its head.

Frog felt his jaw fall open as the someone-or-something blinked in the light of morning. Its yellow eyes were large and oval, its head wide and hairless. And its skin … its skin was *green*. This giant looked more like him than any creature he had seen since his arrival in the Not-So-Ended World – even more than Mr Hoppy the frog.

"I am General Kurg," it said in a thunderous growl – then knelt before Frog. "The Army of a Thousand Sons awaits your order, Prince… "

General Kurg looked up expectantly.

"… Frog?" finished Frog, suddenly doubtful.

"Frog! Interesting choice," said the general. "Welcome to your destiny – Royal Majesty, Lord of all Kingdoms, Rightful Ruler of the World … Prince Frog."

Frog blinked twice. "What the … what?"

The Prince's Fate

"Did you say, *Prince* … Frog?" asked Frog, as the green-skinned giant calling himself General Kurg rose to his feet.

"Why were you living in my lake? It's not allowed," said Princess Rainbow, staring into the giant's yellow eyes. "Mummy says squatters should have their heads chopped off. Do you have any treasure?"

"Have a care, Your Majesty," whispered the wizard, Oldasdust. "My omen hat hasn't been this tight since I lost my house in a game of cards – I fear there is some nasty, dark magic afoot."

General Kurg raised an eyebrow, his hand hovering over his holster.

"Are you all set to give the order, my

prince?" he said, looking down at Frog. "The Army of a Thousand Sons awaits your— Uh, are you aware that you're naked?"

"Yep," replied Frog. "What did you say just then? All that 'Royal Majesty, Lords of all Kingdoms' and such. That's just what Buttercup—"

"Aha! Told you he was a gobbin!" cried Oldasdust. "He's speaking their language!"

"Stop being rude, Greeny," interrupted the princess. "You're not allowed to talk gibby-gobby-goo. I'm the Princess of Everything and I say speak proper English."

"Proper— What are you talking about?" asked Frog, turning to the princess. "Wait, you can't understand him?"

"I can't understand *you*," the princess replied. "I mean, I did then, but not *then* … not when you're talking gobbin gibby-gobby-goo. Half the time you're speaking *their* speak."

Frog turned slowly back to General Kurg and examined him carefully. "Am I speaking gobbin? I didn't even know I was – I mean, I didn't even know I could... How do I know gobbin speak?"

General Kurg tilted his head. "What's a gobbin? How are you communicating with the natives? Where is your Keeper?" he replied.

Frog answered the general's questions with more questions of his own. "Who are you? Why were you living at the bottom of the lake? What was that red light that ka-sploded my brain? And why do you keep calling me 'Prince'?"

"I have woken from *farsleep* with a splitting headache," replied the general. "If this is all a joke, forgive me if I don't see the funny side."

"The funny side of what?" asked Frog.

"By the Void … is your brain in a stink?" gasped General Kurg. "Have these natives been messing with your mind-business?"

"Huh?" Frog said.

"By Kroakas! They have! You're stunk-up something chronic!" grunted General Kurg. "This is *bad*."

"Gibby-gobby-goo!" protested Princess Rainbow. "Speak English, gobbins!"

"You'd better come inside, the doctor will check you over," concluded the general. He pointed up at the great, tendril-legged monolith above them.

"Up in that thing? Yoiks!" replied an excited Frog.

The general led him up the narrow tongue of a stairwell and inside the giant clamshell machine.

"*I* want to go inside!" protested the princess immediately. "*I* want to see the treasure first. I'm the princess..."

"Serves you right for locking me in a cage," tutted Frog.

The general guided him inside the clamshell. "Welcome to the command bipod, my Prince!" he declared.

"Great! What's a bipod?" said Frog, as they made their way through a curved, metal corridor into a large chamber, much like the one Frog had found on the bottom of the lake — but lit red and with an impressive-looking seat in the middle of the room, almost like a throne. Round the walls Frog saw half a dozen smaller but almost-as-impressive-looking versions of General Kurg. They were all busily staring into what looked like mirrors made of light, which seemed to be answering their stares with pictures of the palace ... the gardens ... the gathered crowds...

"Behold his Royal Majesty, Lord of all Kingdoms, Rightful Ruler of this World, Prince ... Frog!" barked General Kurg.

The green-skinned giants immediately turned to face Frog and lifted their fists to their chests. "Hail, Kroak! Hail, Prince Frog!" they cried.

"They're *all* calling me 'Prince'..." said Frog, a cautious smile spreading across his face.

"Kull! Doctor Kull!" barked General Kurg.

A thin, green-skinned giant with a surprisingly large head appeared over Frog's shoulder. She peered at Frog through wide, orange-yellow eyes.

"Ah, yes, I see," she hissed. "This

confirms it."

"Confirms what?" the general barked. "What's his prognosis? Is he stunk up in his brain end? In the name of the Universal Strangulation, tell me, Doctor!"

"Calm yourself, General," the doctor replied. She opened her spindly fingers to reveal a ball of glowing red light. "I have already communed with the *lexicron*."

"That's the light from the bottom of the lake!" declared Frog. "What's a lexicron?"

"'What's a lexicron?'!" By the slurms of Urm! This is what I'm talking about!" howled the general. "All stunk up!"

"The lexicron is suffering some water damage," continued the doctor, "but from what I can glean, our farship was caught in a lightning storm upon entering the planet's atmosphere. We crashed."

"Moons of Moonos!" boomed the general. "Where's the prince's Keeper? Blasted scheming mystic! If the farship was in trouble, why didn't she wake us?"

"We'll probably never know — it appears the keeper was extinguished in the crash," the doctor replied with a shrug. "The prince — the un-hatched royal spawn — somehow floated up to the planet's surface. He hatched *outside* the farship."

"Great suns of Kroakas! Then who kept him alive, if not the Keeper?" the general bellowed.

"Who knows? Only one thing is certain — the prince did not return here until today, when he made contact with the lexicron and woke us from farsleep."

The general clenched both his fists until they made an unpleasant cracking sound.

"How long…?" he said through gritted teeth. "How long have we been asleep?"

"Five kronons," came the doctor's reply. "At least."

"*Five kronons?*" cried General Kurg. "By the Crush! We're behind schedule! We must look like a bunch of untrained *skirns!*"

"It is quite possible King Kroak hasn't yet checked on our progress," mused the doctor. "After all, he does have nine hundred and ninety-nine other planets to worry about…"

"By the Turmoil! We can't take that risk – if the King *does* find out, we'll be turned into protein bars! Or worse … we'll be the laughing stock of the empire!" roared the general. "Well, fix it, Doctor! We can't have a brain-stunk prince!"

"I'm afraid it's not as simple as 'fixing' him, General," the doctor replied.

"The lexicron has transferred our language to him — but little else. He has not been trained. He doesn't even know who he is. To all intents and purposes, our prince is not a prince."

"Would you *please* stop talking about me like I'm not here?" interrupted Frog. "I so *am* a prince! I've been waiting to be a prince for my whole life! I'm ready. I'm readier than ready!"

The general rubbed the top of his bald, green head, blinking his eyes in two directions as he peered at Frog.

"Perhaps the lexicron did get through to you, after all," he said hopefully. "All right then — pay attention!"

The Five-hundred-and
-thirteenth Son

As Frog looked on in confused awe, a dark green world appeared on one of the bipod's picture-mirrors.

"Hey, I've seen that," cried Frog. "That's what I saw when I touched the red light in the lake and my mind went Bwooooooo! Fwaaaah! Stuuufff!"

"*That* is Kroakas, our home planet," the General began. "It is—"

"What's a planet?" asked Frog.

"What's a—? By the Clenched Fist!" growled the general. "It's … a big place. So, we set off from this *big place* and travelled through space to—"

"What's space?" asked Frog.

"It's far away," the general huffed. "We have travelled from a big place far away to reach *this* big place so that—"

"I fell down a waterfall in the sky," interrupted Frog. "Now that was far."

"Can I finish?" the general blurted. "So, we went from that big place to this big place to play our part in King Kroak's grand scheme for the universe."

"What's a universe?"

"Kroak's teeth!" huffed the general. "Look … King Kroak is our supreme leader, the rightful ruler of the birds in the sky, the beasts of the land and the entire universe. He has sworn to conquer a thousand worlds."

"Yoiks…" said Frog, even though he wasn't altogether sure what the general meant.

"As tradition dictates, you were transported here as an egg, to hatch upon this planet," interjected Doctor Kull.

"I *knew* princes hatched from eggs!" Frog exclaimed.

General Kurg reached down to the handle at his side. He drew it out of the holster on his leg – it looked almost like the hilt of a bright red sword, but without a blade. He handed it to Frog.

"Your *sunder-gun*," he said. "A weapon fit for a prince."

"Shined-up just the way I like! What does it do?" said Frog, examining the strange weapon with delight. He used it to scratch his head (causing every Kroakan in the room to shriek in horror) and added, "I *still* don't think I understand how I fit into this."

"You, Prince Frog? By the Right to Smite! You are the spawn of King Kroak – his five-hundred-and-thirteenth son," replied the general. "You have been *chosen* to rule this world."

"Chosen...?" whispered Frog.

General Kurg waited expectantly for more of a response, but none came. He glanced at Doctor Kull, who shrugged and crossed her long fingers. They watched Frog look slowly around the room, as the strange, green-skinned giants peered back at him. Then...

"I knew it! I *knew* I was a prince! I told them!" he cried, fist-punching the air. "This is the best, most excellent day ever — by a million!"

The general breathed a sigh of relief.

"Wait till I tell Buttercup! Wait till I tell Sheriff Explosion! Wait till I tell ... the *princess*." Frog narrowed his eyes. "General Kurg! Here is my first royal command: open the clamshell whatsit and extend the

tongue-stairs! I'm going to have a *word* with Princess Rainbow…" He looked down. "Oh, and could someone get me some clothes?"

The Return of Prince Frog

"I'm bored," said Princess Rainbow from atop the wizard's shoulders. Nothing had happened for a whole five minutes — not since Frog had climbed inside the bipod with General Kurg. "Are my newnicorns fully grown yet? I want to go riding."

"Perhaps we should retreat to the palace, Your Majesty," suggested Oldasdust. "I have a bad feeling about these giant gobbins and their—"

"Dun-dun-duuuuh!" came a cry, as the bipod suddenly reopened. The gathered crowds watched aghast as a troupe of green-skinned, black-clad giants made their way down the stairs one after the other, until a dozen of them towered over the princess and her subjects.

"I *said*, dun-dun-duuuuh!"

The giants parted to reveal Frog, walking slowly down the stairs. He was dressed in his own suit of sleek, oil-black armour, with his new sunder-gun holstered at his side. Round his shoulders he wore a long, crimson cape – and upon his head, an ornate black crown with long, curved horns.

"Behold … me!" he added, swishing his cape dramatically. "How do you like my cutting-edge princely fashion?"

"You look like you're going to a gobbin funeral," giggled Princess Rainbow.

"You'd better watch it, Princess. I had to tell my number-one general here not to give you a *proper* telling-off for locking me in a cage," sneered Frog, pointing up at General Kurg.

"Princess — my omen hat is getting *awfully* tight..." warned Oldasdust.

"So, it turns out I am a prince after all!" Frog continued, putting his hands on his hips. "And I'm a much better prince than you are a princess because *I* come from a far-away *plant* called Kroak. That's in *outer place* at the other end of *very far away*, which means I'm destined to rule over this whole world. In your face, Princess Brain-slow."

"Saying you're a prince doesn't make you a prince," huffed Princess Rainbow. "And it doesn't stop you being a silly *frog*."

"Princess!" coughed Oldasdust. "Do not forget most of our royal army is far from the palace. Perhaps it's better if we do not antagonize the gobbins..."

"OK, here are my first royal decrees ..." continued Frog, adjusting his crown.

"One! Find Sheriff Explosion so he can be my trusty steed again. Two! Let's have a tour of the palace! A proper tour — not just the chamber of farty-smelling pets. Three! Polished sandwiches for everyone! Your prince is starving!"

The princess glared at Oldasdust, who gave a nervous shrug. "It couldn't hurt now, could it…?" he simpered.

The tour of the palace could not have been more awkward — for everyone except a giddy Prince Frog. While he squealed with delight at every new room, statue and feature, the enormous Kroakans had to duck continually to avoid hitting their heads on low beams, and made a point of barging the servants out of the way wherever possible.

"By the Flames of Conquest, this is taking forever!" grunted the general. "We have work to do!"

"Agreed — the more we linger, the closer we get to being turned into snack food," whispered Doctor Kull. "If the prince is not capable of fulfilling his destiny, there are ... alternatives."

Princess Rainbow, meanwhile, refused to say a word, huffing and puffing as an increasingly nervous Oldasdust did his best to maintain decorum.

"And this is the Fourth Grand Ballroom," he exclaimed, as they wandered through a grand, gilded hall. "So called because — well, because we have three other grand ballrooms…"

By the time they returned to the garden, the royal chefs had laid out a lavish banquet for the princess and her surprise "guests".

Amidst the majesty of the formal gardens (and in the shadow of the looming Kroakan bipods) was a long table, filled with a sumptuous royal feast of princely proportions – polished sandwiches, polished fruit, polished cakes and gallons of ruby-red roseberry wine (made with polished roseberries).

With the sun shining brightly and the now fully grown newnicorn herd grazing nearby, everyone sat down. At one end of the table sat the princess, Oldasdust and a host of anxious dignitaries, flanked by Man-Lor and a handful of royal guards. At the other end were General Kurg, Doctor Kull, a few confused Kroakan troops – and one very pleased-with-himself prince.

"Isn't this *great*?" Frog exclaimed, stuffing three gleaming sandwiches into his mouth at once. "And not a turnip in sight!"

He washed down the sandwiches with an entire flagon of roseberry wine, and let out a satisfied *BURRRP*.

"Uh, Prince Frog?" began General Kurg, as a servant nervously offered him a cake. "Is this some sort of strategy to lull the natives into a false sense of security? It's just – the clock is ticking. It is time to *give the order*."

"What order?" said Frog, barely listening as he munched on three cakes at once.

Doctor Kull leaned in to the general. "He is lost to us, General – we must *act*," she whispered. "Unless you want to explain to King Kroak why we are having tea with the natives?"

"What am I supposed to do?" replied the

general, in a less-than-quiet whisper. "He's the prince!"

"We should all go bipod racing after this!" cried Frog obliviously. "We could have a whole royal Olympics!"

At the other end of the table, Princess Rainbow's cheeks were turning as red as the roseberry wine.

"This is *stupid*," she snarled. "How come I'm not allowed any friends, but we have to sit here with gibby-gobby gobbins ... and *him*?"

Oldasdust had been trying to prise his omen hat from his head for the last few minutes. "Gah! Can't. . . get it . . . off!" he whispered. "These gobbins are all sorts of badness. We must be cautious, lest we enrage them! Would you care for some cake, Princess?"

"No," huffed the princess, pushing her plate away. "And you just want to keep the gobbins around because they don't speak — not proper, anyway."

"You know the best thing about these sandwiches? Not even a *hint* of turnip," continued Frog at the other end of the table. "Yoiks! I forgot Buttercup!"

"'Buttercup'?" repeated the general.

"She was right about me all along! Well, sort of," Frog went on. "Where was I up to in my royal decrees — three? No, four! Send my fastest bipod and fetch her — she's at the top of a giant waterfall in the sky on a farty little island. Five! I'll be needing my own newnicorn — uh, *that* one, with the blue mane. Six—!"

"No!" squeaked a voice, with such ferocity that everyone (even the newnicorns) stopped what they were doing. Princess Rainbow had clambered on to the table.

"Princess — wait!" whispered Oldasdust.

"You don't get to make royal rules or anything, *Greeny*," said Princess Rainbow. "You're not a prince and you don't get to decide things and you don't — *don't* — get one of my newnicorns!"

"Silence this … *organism*, Your Majesty — give the order," repeated the general, his hand hovering over his sunder-gun.

"Look, Princess — I'm trying to be nice," said Frog, "'cause we're both full-on royalty and everything. But you can't push me around or drag me about or lock me in a cage any more. I'm a *prince*."

"You're just a prince of stupid, gibby-gobby gobbins!" shouted Princess Rainbow. "And that's not a prince at all."

A hush fell about the table. Frog gritted his teeth so hard his jaw ached. "For the last time, these are not gobbins, they're Kroakans ... and I *am* a prince!" protested Frog. "Look, I have a crown! Why would I have a crown if I wasn't a prince? I have a bunch of goodly loyal outer place soldiers! I have giant royal machine steeds!"

"*Shut up!*" snarled Princess Rainbow, stamping her feet on the table and sending a flagon of roseberry wine crashing to the ground. "You'll never, ever be a prince. You're not anything but a frog ... and Buttercup is a thief who should get her head cut off."

Frog's eyes flooded red and he too leaped up on to the table. "Take that back ... take that back right now," he growled.

"Can't make me," replied the Princess. "I'm a princess."

"Give the order, my prince," said the general. "*Give the order* and no one will question you, ever again. All this will be yours..."

Frog stared at the princess, her cheeks as red as his eyes. He thought of Buttercup ... of the island ... of the vegetable patch ... of everything he'd left behind. Then he looked up at the gleaming white palace and remembered what the rarewolf had told him. It suddenly made sense.

"Others will try and decide your fate, Prince Frog. But you must decide for yourself. You must choose your own destiny."

Frog took a deep breath of warm morning air and looked Princess Rainbow right in the eye. "It's given. I mean, I given it. I mean, give it. *I give the order!*"

The Beginning of the End of the World

"You're not going to regret this, my prince!" cried the general. He got to his feet, framed by the great Kroakan bipods. "The order is given! Begin the End of the World!"

"In your face, Princess Brain-slow!" cried Frog, swishing his royal cape. "Begin the End of the— Wait, what?"

The bipods suddenly burst into life, moving in large, slithering steps, scattering the panicking crowd. They turned slowly towards the palace and glowed so brightly that Frog was forced to look away.

"Fire the sunder-beams!" the general roared.

"Wuh...?" blurted Frog.

A moment later, a beam of green light streaked out from each bipod, accompanied by a shrill metallic shriek. The sunder-beams struck the topmost tower of the palace, which exploded in a burst of flames! A shower of white bricks rained down over the roofs and lower towers, crashing and crumbling on to the garden below.

"My palace!" shrieked Princess Rainbow.

The bipods fired another volley of sunder-beams, destroying three more towers and reducing one of the palace's outer walls to rubble.

"Destroy it! Burn it all!" said General Kurg proudly.

"Uh-oh..." whispered Frog.

"We're under attack!" shouted Oldasdust. He reached into his robe, pulled out a talisman and cast it to the floor.

It exploded in a shower of blue light, covering him and the Princess with a magical protective bubble. "Champion! Guards! To arms!" Oldasdust cried. "Slay these monstrous gobbins!"

"I ... am ... Man-Lor!" cried Man-Lor, drawing his great sword. The guards followed suit and rushed bravely towards the Kroakans.

Frog saw General Kurg take his weapon casually out of his holster. It flashed green and a bright, shrieking beam of light streaked forth, hitting a guard and immediately turning him into a very small quantity of grey dust.

"Man-Lor is going to need bigger sword," said Man-Lor.

"Blast them to atoms! Hail, Kroak!" bellowed General Kurg. With one hand, he upturned the entire table, sending food and diners flying. The remaining Kroakan troopers drew their sunder-guns and opened fire, disintegrating the remaining guards in short order.

"Stop! Stop! What are you doing?" shrieked Frog.

"You gave the order, my prince!" cried the general. "The invasion has begun ... this is the beginning of the End of the World!"

"But ... you can't just ... do that – this isn't what I wanted!" cried Frog. "This isn't good! Princes are good because goodness is princely!"

"'Good'? By the Cosmic Whirlwind! Who taught you these words?" scoffed General Kurg. "Being good has nothing to do with victory! King Kroak commands you to bring about the End of the World!"

"But the world's got all the things I want in it, all the things I've been waiting for!" protested Frog. "Why would I want to get rid of it?"

"Why? So that we might rebuild it in the image of our glorious home world!" replied the general, looking down at Frog. "Because you are Prince Frog! Because it is your destiny!"

The Scorched Earth

As the air filled with the screams of panicking servants, the bipods wheeled away from the palace and began stomping through the panicking crowds, squashing servants hither and thither then blasting everything in sight with their sunder-beams.

"Burn it all! Scorch the earth!" roared General Kurg. He watched the bipods burn the gardens — setting fire to the ground itself. A moment later they took aim upon the fleeing herd of newnicorns.

"Don't you dare..." said the princess, under the protection of Oldasdust's weakening magical sphere. "Don't you dare!"

Green beams of energy streaked forth. Frog watched in horror as the newnicorns burst into flames. Still they ran, wheeling in panic back towards the crowd.

"My newnicorns!" screamed the princess. "Bad gobbins!"

"I love the smell of burning life-forms in the morning," said General Kurg.

"The sphere is weak! We must retreat!" the wizard cried.

A moment later, his protective bubble burst in a shower of blue sparks. Oldasdust quickly flung a whole handful of magical talismans to the ground, creating a flash of blinding light, a wall of water ... even a distractingly large rabbit.

The flaming newnicorns stampeded past, trampling servants and setting light to whatever they touched. Man-Lor scooped up Princess Rainbow in his great hands and he, the wizard and the dozen remaining servants began running for the palace.

"General, shall we pursue?" asked Doctor Kull, firing after them.

"Let them hide! We'll bury them inside!" replied the general. "Bipods!"

The bipods turned back to face the palace and all three began to glow green.

"You can't! They'll die!" cried Frog, grabbing the general's leg. "Stop!"

"Stop, my prince?" said the general. "Why would we stop? We're doing so well."

"I said, no!" roared Frog, loudly enough that the general was shaken from his murderous reverie.

He looked down at Frog. After a moment his rasping laughter echoed around the garden. "Now that's better!" he cried. "See how easily you draw your weapon? Perhaps your training isn't as incomplete as we thought…"

"My what...?" Frog looked at his hand. Without realizing, he had drawn the sunder-gun at his side and was pointing it directly at General Kurg.

"Look, I don't know how they do things on the outer-place plant, but I am your prince and you are my loyal subjects and I *order* you to stop trying to end the world," demanded Frog, holstering his weapon.

"But—" began General Kurg.

"I mean it!" added Frog.

The general let out a grunting sigh. "Can we at least blacken the skies?" he asked.

"That doesn't sound good either," replied Frog.

"No – it's very bad," confirmed the general with a grin.

"Then, no!" cried Frog. "Look, just wait here. I'll go and talk to the princess; I'm sure we can sort this out without blowing anything else up. Then maybe we can rule together! You'll see, it'll be great. Just don't destroy anything else…"

General Kurg, the doctor and the confused Kroakan troops watched their prince hurry into the flaming palace.

"Great Suns of Kroakas! What kind of half-baked apocalypse is this? This pro-peace prince is going to stink up my reputation!" the general hissed.

"Reputation? If you don't destroy this world, we are going to be turned into *food*," hissed the doctor. "This prince is sure to doom us all. Unless…"

"Unless what?" asked the general.

"As of this moment, no one on Kroakas has any idea what transpired here," the doctor continued. "The prince's Keeper was extinguished in the crash … no one knows what happened to the prince. Perhaps … perhaps he could simply perish in battle. Heroically, of course."

"You mean…" The general peered at Doctor Kull. "Doctor, what you're suggesting is … mutiny!"

"What I am suggesting for us, General, is that we make it out of this *alive*," replied the doctor. "After all, the End of the World is the End of the World … with or without a prince."

The Blackened Skies

"Princess?" cried Frog. "Lumps? Old wizard? Anyone?" he called, as he hurried through the palace. He could still hear the crackle and crumble of the burning towers and rubble falling high above them — but at least the Kroakans had stopped blowing things up.

"Princess! I'm sorry about the … about all that!" he cried. "I didn't know they were planning the end of … the … world…"

The scorched earth … the blackened skies … catastrophe. Buttercup had spelled it all out to him before it happened. She spoke the very same words as the general. Could she have known who he really was? And if she did, why didn't she tell him?

He was filled with a sudden sense of

dread – and something that he'd never felt before.

Frog was afraid.

He hurried down corridor after corridor, through a courtyard and down a short flight of stairs, until he found himself in a large, well-stocked kitchen. It was lined with vast stoves and ovens, long tables filled with half-prepared food, and countless pans and utensils hanging from the ceiling.

"Princess! Where are you?" he called again. "Where are—"

"I am Man-Lor!" came a cry. The great barbarian burst out from inside a nearby pantry, swinging his massive sword.

"Yoiks!" screamed Frog, as the sword swung past his face and sliced the table in two. It lodged in the floor and Frog stumbled backwards into the wall.

"Chop him up to bits!" squeaked Princess Rainbow, emerging from the pantry.

"Slay him, Champion!" howled Oldasdust, following behind.

"Bad Greeny!" boomed Man-Lor, swinging his sword again.

Frog ducked out of the way just as the vast blade swung into the wall, inches from his head.

"Wait, stop! I'm not here to be mighty!" cried Frog, as Man-Lor struggled to wrench his sword out of the wall. "This is all a mistake, I don't want to end the world!"

"You blowed my palace to bits," snarled the princess. "You squashed everyone ... you set fire to my newnicorns!"

"That wasn't me! I didn't want any of that!" insisted Frog.

"I wanted us to be friends ... but you're

not my pet any more," hissed the princess, staring him in the face. "And you *still* smell like turnips."

Man-Lor abandoned his sword and clenched his fists. Frog hopped out of the way on to a nearby counter, but Man-Lor was deceptively fast — he swung a great arm backwards, swatting Frog across the kitchen and sending him bouncing to a clumsy halt in front of the princess.

"Listen to me!" said Frog, his head still spinning. "This was just a big mistake… I had no idea what the Kroakans were planning — I only met them today!"

"Chop his head off, Champ'un!" squealed the princess.

Man-Lor tore his mighty sword out of the wall. He charged at Frog, who was still struggling to his feet.

With a "Yoiks!" Frog sprung on mighty legs, back-flipping over the top of Man-Lor as he swung again.

"Man-Lor! Wait!" screamed Oldasdust, but it was too late – Man-Lor's sword was moving too fast to stop. By the time Frog turned, the blade was inches from the princess's head.

There was a flash of green light.

The first thing Frog noticed was that Man-Lor's sword no longer had a blade. He looked down to see the sunder-gun in his hand. He had drawn and fired without thinking, reducing the sword to dust.

"You … you *saved* the princess," said Oldasdust.

"Princes are good…" Frog panted, holstering his sunder-gun. "Goodness is princely."

"You're not good," snarled Princess Rainbow. "You're bad. You blowed up everything!"

"No, I *stopped* it. Do you hear any sunder-beams? I stopped them with an excellent royal order. *Trust me.*"

The pots and pans began to rattle. Then a rumble filled the air and the whole room seemed to darken.

"What the ... what?" said Frog.

The princess headed for the stairs and began *klik-klak*-ing up them before the old wizard could stop her.

"Princess, wait!" Oldasdust cried, as he, Frog and Man-Lor raced after her. They made their way into a library overlooking the gardens, crept up to a window and looked out.

The bipods had indeed stopped firing on the palace. Instead, they had unleashed their sunder-beams upon the sky, blasting into the heavens. The sky churned with impenetrably thick black clouds, which spread like ink stirred into water. They had already blocked out the sun and cast the palace into gloom.

"The blackened skies..." began Frog. "But I gave a princely order ... I told them not to..."

"Liar-head! Now they're doing more badness," hissed the princess in her angriest whisper.

"Prince Frog!" came a cry. Frog peered into the encroaching darkness to see General Kurg and his troops gathered in the garden. "I offer you this one chance," the general continued. "Pledge your undying loyalty to King Kroak and you fulfil your destiny – you can rule the Ended World as its prince. We will destroy this wretched planet together! Refuse and you will be extinguished with *extreme* prejudice. The choice is yours. You have one kron to decide."

"Wait ... they can't extinguish me – can they?" Frog muttered. He felt frozen in a moment of impending doom. He pondered the choice he'd been offered – to be the Prince of the scorched earth ... of the blackened skies ... of the End of the World.

"Pfff ... not *this* prince," he said. He prised the crown from his head and threw it to the ground.

"What did the gobbin say?" asked the princess.

Frog clenched his fists. "Did you ever have one of those days when you think you're a prince, but then you find out you're not, but then it turns out you are, but you're not in the way you wanted so you'd be better off not being a prince in the first place?"

"No," Princess Rainbow replied.

"Well, I did," he said. He turned to face the princess. "Someone told me this was going to happen. He said it was a prophecy. He told me I'd have to make a choice."

"Did he tell you that you were a horrid gobbin who ruined everything?" asked the

princess.

"He *told* me I'd have to choose my own destiny ... and I have," Frog replied. "I'm going to save you. Then, after that, I'm going to save the whole world."

The Excellent Plan to Save the Princess and After That the Whole World

"I do *not* need saving," cried Princess Rainbow. "I'm the Princess of Everything!"

"Well, I'm going to save you anyway," replied Frog, watching the Kroakan troops make their way up the garden. "OK, we're going to need an excellent plan and some skilled-up mightiness." He glanced down at his slick Kroakan armour. "First – there's no way I can save the world dressed like a baddie – it's unprincely."

Frog immediately started undressing.

"Gah! Naked gobbin buttocks! Avert your eyes, Princess!" cried Oldasdust. He wagged a finger at Frog. "Must you insist on exposing

172

yourself at every given opportunity?"

"Man-Lor help reduce nakedness," said the barbarian. He reached behind his back and pulled Frog's catastrophe pants out of his furry loincloth. "Man-Lor jealous of pants because Man-Lor's loincloth itchy..."

"Nice work, Lumps!" said Frog. He reached out to take the catastrophe pants — and noticed his broken stick, still tucked into his belt.

"Basil Rathbone ... I wish you really were a sword," he muttered. He shook his head and pulled on the pants. "Right, the next step is finding Sheriff Explosion..."

"Who?" squeaked Oldasdust.

"My sheep," Frog replied. "He's white and woolly. Looks like a sheep."

"A *sheep*?" repeated the princess. "Who cares about a smelly-head sheep?"

"I do, he's the only trusty steed I've got," replied Frog firmly. "Now, do you know where his is or not?"

"I'm afraid your sheep suffered the fate of all uninvited guests," Oldasdust began. "It was locked in the Tower of Tallness."

"You locked up my steed?" cried Frog, shooting the wizard a withering look. "Where is this tower?"

"It *was* at the top of the palace," huffed Princess Rainbow, crossing her arms. "Until your best-friend gobbins blowed it to bits."

"No … we have to get up there!" Frog cried.

"Go *towards* the destruction? What madness!" Oldasdust protested.

"This is not a dress for going to blowed-to-bits places," confirmed the princess, smoothing her sparkly skirts.

"Well, *I'm* going," Frog replied, attaching his sunder-gun to his catastrophe pants. "And since I'm the only one who is a) dressed for catastrophe, b) has a mighty weapon and c) is a skilled-up prince from outer place, then I reckon you're best sticking with—"

"Time's up, O Prince!" came the general's cry. The Kroakans were striding towards the palace. "Join us and live as a prince, or die a short but immeasurably unpleasant death with the rest of these pitiful creatures!"

"*Now* what is he saying?" tutted the princess.

"Nothing important," replied Frog. "Let's go!"

Frog, Princess Rainbow, the wizard Oldasdust and Man-Lor the barbarian hurried through the burning palace. As they sped across the central courtyard, Frog looked up. He saw the sky seething with coal-black clouds – and the ruin of the Tower of Tallness.

"Hang on, Sheriff," he began. "I'm—"

A sunder-beam streaked past Frog's head. He glanced back to see Kroakan troopers only thirty paces behind them.

"Time's up!" cried General Kurg, firing again. "You made your choice, O Prince! Now surrender to the inevitable!"

"Everyone, move!" Frog cried. With a great push of his legs he sprang into the air, landing on a nearby balcony. "Follow me, Lumps! Use your mighty legs!"

"I am Man-Lor!" confirmed Man-Lor, grabbing Princess Rainbow and Oldasdust and leaping into the air. Though his landings were a little ungainly, Man-Lor managed to keep up with Frog, following him up balcony after balcony until they found themselves on the roof of the palace. Ahead of them was the long rampart and, at its end, the archway to the charred remains of the Tower of Tallness.

"They're coming after us!" yelped Oldasdust, looking down to see the Kroakans scaling the balconies. Frog ushered everyone along the rampart. They hurried through the archway and began to climb the stairs.

"Run!" he said, turning back. He drew his sunder-gun and fired at the rampart again and again until he'd blasted it to rubble, leaving nothing but a plummeting drop to the ground below.

Frog hurried inside, racing and leaping up a zig-zagging flight of stairs. By the time he'd caught up with Man-Lor and his passengers, Frog could see that the top of the tower had been completely destroyed.

"There's nowhere left to go!" screeched Oldasdust, the blackened skies churning above them. "We'll be trapped!"

"We don't have a choice! We have to find Sheriff Explosion!" said Frog. "Also, I may have slightly destroyed our way back."

"What a surprise. Your ex'lunt plan is actually a *stupid* plan," tutted the princess.

"I'm improvising! And this wouldn't *be* the plan if you hadn't locked up my steed!" replied Frog.

He ducked under Man Lor's legs and zig-zagged up the remainder of the stairs until he reached the top ... but the stairwell continued into thin air. There was nothing ... nothing and no one.

"Sheriff Explosion... No!" said Frog, falling to his knees. "I will avenge you! You will be avenged!"

"Baa?"

Frog looked down. Dangling from the jagged remains of the very top step, snagged by its thick woolly coat was...

"Sheriff Explosion!" Frog cried. The sheep gave a *baa* of abject terror. "Man-Lor, give me a hand!"

The great barbarian placed the princess and the wizard on the steps and he and Frog leaned over to grab the sheep. As they looked down, they saw the devastation wrought by the Kroakan attack. Huge areas of the palace and its grounds were in ruins, flaming or charred. In the garden, the bipods continued to blast their sunder-beams into the blackening sky.

"They're coming up the tower!" shouted Oldasdust as Frog and Man-Lor pulled the sheep to (relative) safety. Frog peered down the centre of the tower. A sunder-beam flashed so close to his head that if he'd had ears, he would have lost one.

"They jumped the gap!" he cried, drawing his sunder-gun. "That's mightier leaping than I expected."

"I like how all your ideas are terrible," said Princess Rainbow sarcastically.

Frog ignored her, blasting down the stairwell and sending two Kroakan troopers tumbling to the ground.

"By the Doom Bringers! Are you sure the boy hasn't been trained, Doctor?" said the general, watching his troopers plunge to their doom from halfway up the tower. "He's taking to battle like a *glork* to water."

"Then perhaps we should stop toying with him and do this the easy way," hissed Doctor Kull.

"Fine!" grunted the general. "But you're digging his body out of the rubble."

At the top of the tower, Frog fired another volley of sunder-beams. When no one fired back, he dared to peek over the edge of the stairwell.

"They're retreating!" he said. "I did it! In your *face*, Princess Brain-slow. Who's the most skilled-up excellent prince ever? Me is who!"

"Uh, Greeny?" began Man-Lor.

"See, that's how it's done!" continued Frog. "While you sit around crying into your tiara, I'm bringing on the big-time mightiness and—!"

"Greeny!" boomed Man-Lor. He was pointing over the edge of the tower into the garden.

"*What?*" sighed Frog.

Everyone rushed to the edge and peeked over. The bipods had stopped blasting the sky ... and turned towards them.

"See? We *are* going to die — *told* you so," noted the princess.

Frog rubbed his temples, desperately trying to divine some excellence from his princely brain.

"Oldasdust, have you got any of those magic whatjamacallits left?" he asked.

As the bipods took aim, Oldasdust reached into his robe and dug out the last of his enchanted talismans.

"Only two," he said. "One *All Change* transformation stone and my last *Sphere of the Year* protection stone ... that I was saving for a special occasion."

"I think this counts," said Frog, picking up Sheriff Explosion.

"Very well — everyone gather round!" Oldasdust shrieked. He held the protection stone above his head as everyone huddled behind him. Frog squinted as the bipods began to glow…

"Do it!" Frog roared. "Do it now!"

"Gah!" cried Oldasdust again, and cast the talisman on to the step as the sunder-beams fired. There was a flash of shimmering blue light — and a moment later what remained of the tower was obliterated in a shower of rubble.

The Mighty Sword

In the moment before the remainder of the tower was disintegrated, Oldasdust's talisman created a perfect bubble of impenetrable blue energy around him and his companions. The Sphere of the Year flew through the air, propelled by the force of the exploding tower. The sphere contained, in reverse order of height:

Sheriff Explosion the sheep

Princess Rainbow

Prince Frog

The wizard Oldasdust

Man-Lor the barbarian

The bubble arced through the air, clearing the remains of the palace before plummeting downward. The sphere's passengers watched in horror as the ground rushed towards them...

"Baa!"

"Stupid Greeny!"

"Yoiks!"

"Gah!"

"No one ever read Man-Lor's poetry..."

A moment later, the sphere crashed and exploded in a shower of sparks. Its occupants were sent scattering in all directions.

"What the ... what?" said Frog, still clinging on to Sheriff Explosion as he scrambled to his feet. "Where did we land?" He looked around and realized they had crashed on the palace bridge.

It occurred to Frog that it could only have been a few days since he had first crossed the bridge to reach the palace, but it seemed like a lifetime ago.

"Is everyone all right?" Frog cried. He turned towards the burning wreckage of the palace to see Man-Lor get up and dust himself off. "Lumps! Where's the princess? Where's—"

"Oldasdust!"

The princess's cry was desperate. Man-Lor stood aside, and Frog spotted Oldasdust's tall hat lying on the bridge. Then he saw Princess Rainbow, hunched over the old wizard where he lay next to his hat.

"Pr-princess…" muttered Oldasdust, as Frog rushed over to them. "I think … I think I may have broken something important upon landing."

"You're all magic and old like the sea — you'll be all right," said Princess Rainbow hopefully.

"Gah … I fear I am not built for what is to come…" he began with a pained sigh.

"I am just a man, with a man's courage ... but *you* ... you can save us all..."

Oldasdust pointed his finger slowly.

"Who, me?" asked Princess Rainbow.

"No..." replied Oldasdust.

"Me?" asked Man-Lor.

"No..." wheezed Oldasdust.

"Baa?" said Sheriff Explosion.

"No! Him!" gasped Oldasdust, pointing at Frog. "Come closer, Frog. I knew you were important ... from the very moment I— Actually, I had no idea. But still ... I know now that you are ... good. Protect the princess. Where I have failed ... in my promise, you must succeed. Promise me, Frog. Promise me ... you will protect her."

"I—" began Frog.

"I don't need protecting! And I don't need saving!" the princess interrupted.

Oldasdust reached inside his robe for his last talisman — a simple stone with a small curved symbol carved on its face.

"Frog ... your stick — hold it aloft," he coughed, waving his hand weakly.

"Basil Rathbone?" replied Frog, taking the broken stick off his belt. "He's — *it's* — just a stick."

"I'll be the judge ... of that," the wizard wheezed. The charm in his hand seemed to melt into sparkling, shimmering dust, which floated up and surrounded Frog's stick in an aura of light. Frog's wide eyes grew wider still as the stick began to glow — and change.

"Yoiks!"

Within moments, the stick was no longer a stick. Indeed, the very thought that it had ever been a stick was suddenly absurd. It was a *sword* with a long, silver blade that glinted with light and magic. Its fine, sculpted hilt curved round Frog's hand, and the handle immediately felt as much an extension of his arm as his sunder-gun.

"A sword ... fit for a prince," wheezed Oldasdust. "It will cut ... through anything ... so watch your fingers."

"Basil Rathbone ... you look amazing!" cried Frog, a beaming smile spreading across his face. "This is the best, most excellent royal present ever! Thanks, old wizard!"

Oldasdust turned to Princess Rainbow, wincing with pain. "I'm sorry, Princess – I failed you. Please tell your parents ... I tried. And for what it's worth ... I thought you should be allowed ... friends."

"I don't want you to go," said Princess Rainbow, her eyes filling with tears. "I'm the princess and I *order* you to be all right."

But the wizard Oldasdust did not obey the princess's command. He took a last breath and vanished into smoke. All that remained were his robes and one very tall hat.

The Battle on the Bridge

Silence fell over the bridge as everyone tried to take in what had just happened.

Princess Rainbow hugged the old wizard's empty robes. She turned to Frog, tears streaming down her face. "This is your fault..." she hissed.

"I-I was trying to save us..." began Frog.

"You couldn't save anything! You're the most horrid thing there ever was!" insisted the princess. She grabbed at Frog's sunder-gun, tearing it from the holster and shoving it in Frog's face. "The wizard's gone and it's all your fault!"

"I'm sorry!" cried Frog, staring down the gun barrel. "I'm trying my best. I didn't even know there *was* a world last week.

I thought that— Wait, do you even know how to use that?"

"Yes, I do know!" snapped the princess. "I'm going to extinguish *you*! Then you'll be sorry..."

"Gobbins!"

Frog and Princess Rainbow spun round to see Man-Lor pointing at the palace gates. The booming sound of shattering walls suddenly filled the air. Boom followed boom ... closer and louder, until the outer gates of the palace were smashed to pieces, sending the great doors flying through the air.

Frog ducked just in time as one of the doors soared over his head and crashed into the moat. By the time he looked up, all three bipods had emerged from the wreckage of the palace gates.

"Princess, could we discuss you

extinguishing me *after* we've been extinguished by the outer-place invaders?" he suggested.

Sheriff Explosion and Man-Lor huddled round as the towering machines stepped forward on their writhing, metal legs and loomed over them.

"Still alive? By the Hordes of Hyperspace, I'm impressed!" said a voice.

Frog watched General Kurg, Doctor Kull and the remaining six Kroakan troopers clamber and leap over the devastated gates. "Perhaps there is something about you after all, Prince Frog…"

"It's too late for that now," insisted the doctor. "It's him or us."

The general's face hardened. He drew his sunder-gun and the troopers followed suit. Frog's eyes darted about. There was no way they could outrun the bipods across the bridge — and the only other way to escape was over the edge, into a chasm that looked altogether bottomless. Frog felt suddenly alone. He drew his sword...

Then he felt a slight tingle in his toes.

"What the ... what?" he whispered.

The sensation was unmistakable. He looked down at his feet, then up into the ink-black sky.

"Listen for the thunder ... look for the lightning!" the rarewolf had told him. *"I will help you, if I can..."*

"The toes knows!" said Frog, a half-smile flashing across his face. He gripped his sword tightly and turned to General Kurg. "Hey! I'm opening a shop that only sells crushing defeat — and you're my first customers!" he cried. "I'm going to fight you till I've got no mightiness left!"

"Then you shall not last long," growled the general — and aimed his sunder-gun.

KA-BOOOOOM!

All at once, thunder clapped, rain poured and lightning struck! The lightning bolts darted out of the churning, ink-black clouds, striking all three bipods with such force that they sparked and shook.

"Kroak's teeth!" yelled the general. "We're under attack!"

"Man-Lor, get them out of here! Run!" Frog cried.

As Man-Lor grabbed Princess Rainbow and Sheriff Explosion, Frog held his breath and triggered his camouflage — in a moment, only his catastrophe pants and sword were visible.

"Did you see that? He's mastered the *Kroak cloak*! The prince has the power of the Keepers!" the general howled. "Open fire! Blast him! Aim for his pants!"

The Kroakans fired through the torrent of rain at their all-but-invisible enemy. As sunder-beams whizzed past his head, Frog raced towards the closest bipod and sprang into the air on his mighty legs. He leaped towards one of the bipod's massive metal tendrils and swung his sword with all his might. The magical blade sliced through the alien metal like it was a rotten turnip sandwich. Sparks flew from the severed limb as it toppled to the ground.

Frog grinned. *I'm sorry I ever doubted you, Basil Rathbone!*

"By the Imperial Forehead!" the general cried.

Frog spiralled through the air and landed on the bridge. He skidded to a halt, sliding through a slick of rain as more lightning streaked down from the sky. He glanced back to see Man-Lor racing towards the other end of the bridge with the princess and his trusty steed in his arms ... then he heard a strained metallic creak fill the air. The one-legged bipod began to waver and stagger towards the edge of the bridge...

"My favourite bipod!" shrieked the general, as he watched it tumble over the edge and plummet into the darkness below. His eyes all but glowed with rage. "By the Boot of Oppression! Someone extinguish that prince!"

"It's no good! Between the rain and the Kroak cloak, he might as well be a *ghost*," snarled the doctor, wiping her eyes in the driving rain.

"Then we turn him into one!" General Kurg cried. "Bipods, blast the bridge! Send him into the chasm!"

The two remaining bipods wheeled round, their sunder-beams aglow, and took aim.

"Yoiks..." Frog muttered. His eyes darted left and right, but there was no way to get across the bridge in time. He took a deep breath and leaped into the air. The searing, shrieking sunder-beams shattered the ground beneath him, sending rubble tumbling into the chasm.

Frog soared over the top of the nearest bipod, landing roughly on its smooth, rain-slick shell and sliding to a clumsy halt. He watched the great machines blast the middle of the bridge to smithereens, leaving either end jutting out over the dark abyss. Despite his near-death experience, Frog smiled –

with the centre of the bridge gone, there was no way the bipods could reach the princess, Man-Lor and Sheriff Explosion on the other side.

"That *must* have extinguished him," the general began, trying to see through the rain. "No one could have survived—"

"I see him!" snarled Doctor Kull. "Up there!"

From atop the bipod, Frog saw the doctor point directly at him. He looked at his hands and realized that he had lost concentration – he was no longer camouflaged.

"Uh-oh," he squeaked.

"By the Galactic Wedgie! Why will this prince not die?" cried the general.

Frog clung on to the bipod for dear life, as the other wheeled round to face him.

"What are you waiting for? Incinerate

him!" the general roared.

"Not again…" muttered Frog. He scrambled to his feet and leaped into the air, flinging himself at the other bipod as it fired. As the first bipod exploded, Frog skidded helplessly along the second's surface, jabbing his sword into the bipod's shell to steady himself.

"We're losing machines of mass destruction by the *mikron*," huffed the doctor, as they watched the blasted bipod stumble and sway, its body consumed with flames. It lurched unsteadily one way then the other, then it staggered backwards…

"It's going down! Move!" ordered the general, leaping at the doctor and knocking her clear. He glanced back to see the bipod fall to the ground on top of the Kroakan troopers, squashing them flat.

"My troops! My loyal, nameless troops!" he shrieked. "By the Void, Frog, you will *pay* for this…"

With a leap as mighty as Prince Frog's, General Kurg propelled himself into the air and landed squarely on top of the remaining bipod.

"You're mine now, O Prince. There's nowhere to run," the general growled.

Frog pulled his sword out of the bipod and brandished it defiantly. "You don't scare me!" he replied, although he wasn't sure he meant it. "I'm going to chew you up like a turnip sandwich and then spit you out like … a turnip sandwich!"

"I was wrong about you, Prince Frog — you truly are a mighty son of Kroak!" laughed the General. "I will do you the honour of a fair fight."

With that, he threw his sunder-gun over the edge of the bipod, sending it spinning into the chasm below.

Frog looked down at his sword. After a moment he shrugged and jammed it back into the top of the bipod. He rolled his neck and clenched his fists. "Let's do this."

The Duel

As rain poured and thunder clapped, Frog and General Kurg circled each other on the surface of the bipod. Frog stared into the general's rage-red eyes, fear suddenly gripping him like a vice. He glanced down to the chasm below.

"Die, O Prince!"

General Kurg raced at Frog, who darted out of the way of his swinging fist. The general swung again and again. After nimbly avoiding two more blows, Frog saw his chance – and swung his fist hard into the general's stomach.

"OWW!" cried Frog. It was like hitting stone. He looked up to see the general smile, before swatting Frog across the surface of the bipod. The blow dazed Frog so much he could barely see. He shook his head and spat out a tooth.

"Who knows? I might even end up with a promotion after this," said the general, edging carefully towards Frog. "The general who conquered a planet without a prince…"

He grabbed Frog by the neck and lifted him into the air. Frog swung his fists as hard as he could, raining blows upon the general's face — but they seemed to bother him even less than the rain. The general took Frog in both hands and raised him above his head, before sending him crashing down on to the unforgiving metal.

Frog felt his bones rattle as he saw the general's fist rushing towards his face. He rolled out of the way, the punch missing him by inches — and dragged himself to his feet. Out of the corner of his eye he saw the general lunge again and felt his boot strike him hard in the stomach.

Frog was sent careering across the bipod's surface. He reached out in the desperate hope of steadying himself – and his hand found the hilt of his sword. His momentum dragged the sword through the metal, tearing through the shell and sending flaming sparks bursting forth. The bipod immediately started to stagger and sway.

"What is it with you and wrecking bipods?" growled General Kurg, trying to stay on his feet as the bipod reeled. "You've stunk up the stabilizers! We're going down!"

Frog slid his sword into his belt as the great machine tumbled into the chasm. He heard himself cry, "Abandon ship!" and he and the general leaped into the air, propelling themselves across the gap in the bridge.

Frog felt time slow down as he reached for the other side...

"EuOOooff!" Frog grabbed hold of the edge of the bridge and clung on by the tips of his fingers. The general landed clumsily next to him. He clawed at the crumbling stone, desperate to hold on, but his own weight dragged him, screaming, off the edge...

"General!" Frog cried. He reached out and grabbed General Kurg by the hand. "Hang on! I've got you!"

Frog held on with all his might, but it was not enough. He felt his grip weaken ... his fingers slip...

"Got you, Greeny!" came a cry, and Frog saw a huge, familiar hand wrap round his wrist. In the next moment, he and the general were hauled up to safety.

Frog rolled on to his back and tried to

catch his breath, though every gasp made him want to cry out in pain. He opened his eyes ... and saw the face of Man-Lor smiling back at him.

"Thanks ... Lumps," puffed Frog, weakly attempting a smile.

A moment later, Princess Rainbow and Sheriff Explosion came into view.

"Have you finished saving us yet?" asked Princess Rainbow. She helped him slowly to his feet as Man-Lor pinned General Kurg to the floor with a great fur-booted foot.

"Get your stinking foot off me, you — you native!" cried the general.

"I am Man-Lor," replied Man-Lor with a grin.

"Do you want this back, Greeny?" asked the princess, holding Frog's sunder-gun out to him. "I don't want to extinguish you any more."

"That's good to know," Frog replied as he reached for the gun. "I've had enough extinguishing to last— uuUHH!"

Frog was sent hurtling to the ground. Something had landed on top of him, driving him into the stone.

"Did someone call for a doctor?"

It was Doctor Kull. She had leaped across the gap in the bridge and now stood over the stunned Frog, her sunder-gun drawn.

"You think you get to decide my fate, Frog? I will *not* end up as a protein bar," hissed the doctor. She aimed at Frog's head. "Foolish prince – you should have stayed inside that egg…"

"That was *my* egg!" cried Princess Rainbow. She looked down at the sunder-gun in her hands – and threw it as hard as she could. It flew through the air and bounced off the doctor's brow.

Doctor Kull howled in pain and surprise. She stumbled backwards towards the bridge's shattered edge and plummeted into the chasm. Her blood-curdling cry echoed through the mist and the darkness – and then faded to silence.

The princess picked up the sunder-gun and carried it back over to the sprawled-out Frog. "*Told* you I knew how to use it," she tutted.

The Calm After
the Storm

The storm passed as quickly as it had arrived, leaving Frog in no doubt that the rarewolf had come to his aid.

By the time the last drop of rain had fallen, Frog was back on his feet. Man-Lor and the princess had already tied up General Kurg. In what the princess considered to be a fitting tribute to a great wizard, they had bound him with Oldasdust's robes. Even Sheriff Explosion played his part – by chewing lazily on the general's boot.

"You think this is over, Frog?" said the general. "You think King Kroak will let this planet go unconquered? You haven't saved anything! Don't you see? You have only delayed the inevitable! This is just the beginning! The End of the World is upon you, Prince Frog!"

"What's he saying now?" huffed the princess.

Frog swallowed hard. "Nothing important," he replied.

"Gibby-gobby-goo-talking gobbin," tutted the princess. "Pull the robes tighter, Champ'un."

"Baa," agreed Sheriff Explosion.

Frog made his way back towards the edge of the bridge. He stared up at the ruined palace, not quite able to believe what had happened.

"Mummy and Daddy are going to be *really* grumped about this," sighed the princess, following behind. "You prob'ly shouldn't be here when they get back."

"I really am sorry," replied Frog. "And *thanks* for saving me from the evil outer-place doctor, and for not extinguishing me when you had the chance."

The princess shrugged. "You saved me too, I s'pose…" she said. After a moment she added, "And it was nice to have someone to talk to for a bit … Prince Frog."

"Just 'Frog' is fine," replied Frog. "I don't think I want to be an excellent royal prince any more."

"What are you going to do if you're not a prince?" asked the princess. "Are you going to live in a pond on a lily pad?"

Frog let out the smallest of laughs, even though it made every bone in his body hurt. He turned away from the palace and towards the Not-So-Ended World. Beyond the patch of blackened skies, bright shafts of golden light shone down over valleys, hills, mountains, seas — a whole world that he had thought was ended, a world that he might just have saved.

He puffed out his chest as far as he could manage. "First, I'm going to go home," he replied, staring out over the mountain. "Buttercup will probably be wondering where I've been all this time and I have a lot of questions to ask her. I think she knows more than … she … wuh?"

On a distant rocky outcropping, Frog spotted a large, dark shape, staring directly at him.

"The rarewolf!" he said. He managed to lift his arm enough to give a painful wave. "Thanks for the bad weather!" he cried.

The rarewolf seemed to nod, then it turned slowly to the side — and Frog spotted something on its back.

Someone was riding it — as if it was a trusty steed. Frog peered more closely.

The figure was tall and slender, with long, dark robes flowing in the wind. It had large, bulbous, yellow eyes and a smooth, hairless head. And its skin…

Its skin was *green*.

"What the … what?" said Frog, as the rarewolf and its passenger sloped off down the mountain. Frog shook his head.

"Baa."

Frog looked down to see Sheriff Explosion peering up at him.

"It's been nice knowing you, too, Sheriff," said Frog. "But you're free to go. Now I'm not doing the whole royal prince thing, I can't ask you to be my trusty steed."

"Baa?" replied Sheriff Explosion.

"Maybe it wants to be your trusty steed anyway," suggested Princess Rainbow. "'Cause it's stupid."

A smile spread across Frog's face.

"You know what, Princess? Maybe you're right," he replied. "Maybe he's just proud to carry the outer-place, invader-defeating saviour of probably the world on his back! Let's go, Sheriff Explosion!"

With that, Frog leaped on to his trusty steed. "To the island! Giddy up! Giddy, I say!"

Sheriff Explosion did not move.

"Oh, come on, we've been through this — what sort of trusty steed doesn't do any steeding?" said Frog.

After a moment, he sighed and hopped off. "Fine — but I am *not* carrying you," Frog huffed.

"Baa," said the sheep.

The Advenchur continues in

FROG THE BARBARIAN

Availabul Summer 2014

Hear's a bit of it!

So Frog had saved the Prinsess and probubly the whole wurld. It was a big day.

After that Frog said goodbye to the Prinsess and the little bit of palase that was left. He desided he didn't ewer want to rool anything any more. He didn't ewer want to sit on a throne in the palase and he didn't ewer want to distroy the wurld like an alien space invader.

He was not going to do any of those things, ewer again. So what was he going to do?

The Sixty-Four-Thousand-Polished-Sandwiches Question

Frog closed his book. He pulled his red cloak around him and began to chew on the piece of chalk in his hand.

"That's the sixty-four-thousand-polished-sandwiches question, isn't it?" he said. "What am I going to do now?"

He sat up and looked around. It was a bright, frosty morning and both the sun and moons hung in the sky. To the east was a forest of blue-leaved trees, overlooked by a crescent-shaped rock. To the west, rolling crimson-red hills gave way to a range of jagged, snow-covered mountains. Frog watched a family of mammoth oak-lice make their way across the distant horizon, as ancient as the trees they carried on their backs. Nearby, yapping bark larks dived for whistle fish in a trickling river. Frog glanced over to see a woolly white sheep grazing lazily on the riverbank.

"What would you do, Sheriff Explosion?" Frog asked, hopping over to his trusty steed. He tore a clump of frosted, lime-green grass from the bank and fed it to the sheep. "I mean, if you didn't want to be a prince but you were still definitely the most excellent, skilled-up outer space someone in Kingdomland and probably the whole, entire universe? Would you just let all that mightiness go to waste?"

"Baa," replied Sheriff Explosion before chewing on the grass.

"Neither would I," replied Frog. He peered into the river and saw his reflection looking expectantly back at him. His round, hairless head and bulbous, yellow eyes seemed strange and otherworldly ... his bright green skin decidedly extraterrestrial. Frog realised how much like the aliens he must look - how like the Kroakan invaders who, two days earlier, had tried to destroy the world. He wasn't sure he liked what he saw.

"Buttercup will know what I'm supposed to do – she always knows how to make the right choice," he concluded. "I've met princesses, wizards, aliens ... and yet Buttercup's still my only real friend around here."

"Baa?" Sheriff Explosion bleated.

"You're a trusty steed – that's different," replied Frog.

"Baa," the sheep sighed.

"Anyways, I need to tell Buttercup the world hasn't ended!" Frog added. "So, we follow the river until we reach the giant waterfall in the sky — then it's just a long, mighty swim to the top and a quick froggy-paddle to the farty little island. Pfff... Never thought I'd be going ... back ... wuh?"

Frog had spotted something in the river — a small, black shape submerged under the water. At first he thought it was some sort of turtle-stone ... but as he peered closer he realised it was a reflection. Frog spun around and looked up. A small, oil-black orb floated in mid-air above him. It rotated constantly on its axis, emitting a low, breathy hum and sparking with green light.

"Baa?" said Sheriff Explosion.

"What is that?" murmured Frog as the spinning orb buzzed around him like a bumbleflea. Suddenly it swooped under his legs and over his head — so close that he was sure it would hit him. It stopped dead in the air, inches from Frog's face. It seemed to be looking at him. A chill ran down Frog's spine. The orb was oddly familiar. He reached out a hand to touch it.

WHiiiiiiSHT – SHUNG!

Frog felt something whistle past his head, and the orb vanished before his eyes. He turned to see it pinned against a tree, a long arrow protruding from the trunk.

"Yoiks…" squeaked Frog. He edged towards the tree as the orb sparked and fizzed its last. Cautiously, he reached out and stroked the arrow's feathered tip. "Yoiks! That's some skilled-up arrow action … unless it was aimed at me. Hey! Was that aimed at me?"

Frog looked behind him – and then up and up, over the top of the blue forest, following the arrow's trajectory. There, standing on the edge of the high, crescent shaped rock…

"The rarewolf!" Frog cried. The great, grey wolf stood motionless, as huge as a horse. Squinting, Frog could make out a slender, green-skinned figure perched upon its back. Frog had seen the figure once before – albeit from afar – sitting atop the rarewolf moments after Frog saved Princess Rainbow and probably the whole world. But this time he could see exactly what it was.

A Kroakan.

An outer space alien invader.

At first he thought it must be General Kurg (the only Kroakan to survive the invasion attempt) but the General was locked up in what remained of the royal palace. And anyway, this Kroakan was female and more slender than any of the Kroakan invaders. A chill ran down Frog's spine.

"What the … what?" he whispered. The rarewolf huffed and began to slope down the outcropping. The Kroakan rider adjusted a longbow on his shoulder. Then he turned back and gave Frog a nod.

"Wait! Come back!" Frog cried. He turned to his sheep. "My big bucket of questions is bursting, Sheriff! Who is that mystery Kroakan? Why is she riding the rarewolf? Why has the rarewolf not eaten her? What the bumbles is going on? Unless— Wait! Unless she's put some outer space alien evil eye on the rarewolf and turned him into her trusty slave. Full-on badness! Grab your things, Sheriff Explosion!"

Frog quickly collected all his worldly goods. They numbered:

One journal, in which Prince Frog recorded his adventures in the third person

Words ending in -able

a	g	o	c	a	b	l	o	p	f	b	c
p	r	p	o	e	q	p	a	m	a	r	o
p	e	e	n	d	w	o	t	e	s	e	m
l	l	r	s	r	e	l	o	i	h	a	f
i	b	a	i	t	r	r	l	a	i	k	o
c	a	b	d	s	f	t	e	m	o	a	r
a	n	l	e	t	h	y	r	a	n	b	t
b	o	e	r	h	u	a	a	g	a	l	a
l	s	a	a	y	i	s	b	i	b	e	b
e	a	b	b	u	l	d	l	l	l	h	l
e	e	l	l	i	o	f	e	c	e	b	e
r	r	d	e	p	e	n	d	a	b	l	e

applicable
tolerable
operable
considerable
dependable
comfortable
reasonable
perishable
breakable
fashionable

One sunder-gun, Prince Frog's outer space alien invader ray pistol One invincible magic sword (named Basil Rathbone) given to Frog by a dying wizard with a very tall hat

Frog holstered his sword and sunder-sun and shoved his journal into the back of his Catastrophe Pants – his (rather tatty) End of the World-proof shorts.

"Let's go, Sheriff – the chase is on!" cried Frog – and disappeared into the forest.

"Baa…" sighed Sheriff Explosion.

Have you read...

In CASTLE
GROTTESKEW
something BIG
is about to happen...

...to someone SMALL.

Join a mad professor's forgotten
creation as he steps out of the
shadows into the adventure
of an almost-lifetime...

Guy Bass

STITCH HEAD

The Pirate's Eye

Someone
SMALL
is about
to set sail
on a
BIG
adventure.

Join a mad professor's forgotten
creation as he prepares for an
almost-life on the high seas.

Guy Bass

STITCH HEAD

The Ghost of Grotteskew

Someone
SMALL
is about to
discover a
BIG
secret.

Join a mad professor's
forgotten creation as he fights
for his heart and soul…

Guy Bass

STITCH HEAD

THE SPIDER'S LAIR

Someone
SMALL
is about to
get into
BIG
trouble.

Join a mad professor's
forgotten creation as he gets
caught up in a web of mystery…

Also by Guy Bass:

Guy Bass is an award-winning author whose children's books include *Secret Agent: Agent of X.M.A.S*, the *Dinkin Dings* series and, most recently, the highly acclaimed *Stitch Head* series. In 2010, *Dinkin Dings and the Frightening Things* won the CBBC Blue Peter Award in the 'Most Fun Story with Pictures' category. Guy's books have also won a number of local book awards.

Guy has also written plays for both adults and children. He has previously been a theatre producer, illustrator and has acted his way out of several paper bags.

Guy lives in London with his wife. He enjoys long walks on toast and the smell of a forgetful sparrow.